Elizabeth's False Fiancé

A PRIDE AND PREJUDICE VARIATION

BRIAR MASTERSON

One

Dread washed over me as I lay upon my bed and stared up at the white canopy above. Dread seemed a somewhat stark emotion for such an early hour of the morning, but it was all I could feel as I listened to the noise in the house.

It was early enough that my younger sisters would not wake for a precious few hours yet, and still more time before our mother would rouse herself from her chambers and venture downstairs for tea.

She would take her breakfast in bed, as she always did, and Lydia would complain about not being allowed to sleep later... as she did every morning regardless of the hour.

Jane was already awake, and though she was trying to be quiet, it was impossible for me to return to my slumber. My mind was awake now, and the longer I lay there, the more time I would have to conjure a fresh assumption as to what awaited us that day.

What new scheme had our mother concocted to see us all wed as soon as possible?

"Lizzy," Jane murmured. "Are you awake?"

"I am," I replied.

"You have not been yourself lately," she observed as she came over to the bed. I sat up and pulled my knees up to my chest.

"You are already dressed," I said, hoping to change the subject, but Jane's brow furrowed and I let out a sigh. "You are quite correct, I have not been feeling myself in recent weeks."

"It is not Kitty's engagement is it?" Jane asked.

"Certainly not," I said with a smile. "I am beyond excited for our dear sister. I do believe that she will be very happy with Mr. Mason."

Jane sat down on the edge of my bed. "I do hope that Mama will... not be in such a hurry to find more husbands for us."

I tried not to laugh, but could not help myself. "Indeed, I do believe that Mama will be emboldened by this victory! I had almost hoped that Kitty would not accept Mr. Mason's proposal—if only so that we both might be spared Mama's scheming for another season."

Jane's smile was faint. "There is nothing in the world that would have prevented Kitty from accepting that proposal, and you well know it."

"I do, indeed. Though I am not quite certain that Lydia is as enthusiastic about the match."

Jane's nose wrinkled. "She has been rather—"

"Horrid?"

Jane nodded. "She has. Oh, Lydia, why is she so cruel to Kitty?"

"I believe," I said, "and I may be correct in this, that our dear Lydia had her own designs on Mr. Mason."

"Do you really believe so? He is... he is certainly nothing like the usual sort of gentleman she favors..."

"Oh, no?" I asked. "I thought that one of the only criteria need be that Kitty found him handsome."

Jane covered her mouth to smother her laughter. She knew as well as I did that Lydia did not do anything without careful calculation as to how it might benefit her, or cause poor Kitty some distress.

In some things they were firm partners, and in others... Lydia would not be satisfied unless Kitty were vexed in some way.

"Will you truly not tell me what is weighing on you?" Jane asked.

"There is nothing to tell," I said with a sigh as I pushed back the coverlet.

"Mama has been growing desperate of late," Jane ventured. "Lady Lucas has even mentioned it—"

"That does not surprise me at all," I said and then yawned and stretched before I plunged my hands into the bowl of washing water.

"She said that Mama had been talking of marrying either you or I to the next gentleman who came to Longbourn to see Papa," Jane continued.

"Did she," I murmured as I bent forward over the bowl to wash my face. Anything to avoid looking at my sister.

"Does that not bother you?"

Did Jane suspect that my unease with the notion was something more than the sudden realization that I was not eager to marry?

"I cannot say that I am surprised that Mama has been talking of it," I said lightly. "Although, it must be said that I have never known Mama's schemes to amount to anything. And she has been talking of marrying us to any gentlemen that showed interest for the last two years."

"This is also true," Jane laughed. "I daresay Mr. Mason was fortunate in the fact that he already had a fondness for Kitty, which made Mama's focus on him all the easier when it came to securing his proposal—although I did wish that it would have been more romantic... for Kitty's sake at least."

"And who would she intend for us to marry? If Lady Lucas has caught wind of it, I should think that every available gentleman in Hertfordshire would have heard the rumors by now and will have departed for London before they can come within sight of Longbourn!"

Jane laughed and I pressed a linen cloth to my cheeks to dry my face and hide my pained expression from my sister's gaze.

"A great relief," Jane said. "There is not one gentleman in Hertfordshire that I could bear being married to."

"Oh, Jane, are you quite certain," I teased her. "Surely one of Mr. Crane's clerks has caught your eye!"

Jane threw a pillow at me, but I dodged out of the way and it landed harmlessly upon the carpet beside me.

"Do you not have any preferences?" Jane asked. Her eyebrow rose as she looked at me. looking at me and raising an eyebrow.

"Indeed I do not," I replied with a snort.

"But, Lizzy—"

"But, Jane," I countered. "Perhaps I do not wish to be married at all! Perhaps my plan for the future is to follow you around England to play governess to your ten children and teach them to play the pianoforte very poorly and dance only to seven very specific tunes..."

"Lizzy, you are being very unreasonable," Jane said, but her smile was genuine. We both knew that I would be very happy if I never married at all.

"You know what Mama says," I declared as I pulled a clean chemise over my head. "A single man in possession of a good fortune, must be in want of a wife."

Jane laughed. "Indeed, it is surely a truth that is surely universally acknowledged."

"But what Mama does not say, and perhaps it is because she does not know... but it is a great misfortune indeed to assume that a single young lady without a fortune is in want of a husband. I, for example, would like nothing of the sort."

Jane rose from the bed and grabbed the pillow she had thrown at me. She set it back upon the bed and pulled the coverlet back into place as I selected a plain muslin dress from the wardrobe we shared.

"And how, pray, will you explain that to Mama?" she asked.

I frowned at my reflection in the vanity mirror. "I have not yet decided," I said.

"Well," Jane said as she smoothed down her skirts and patted at her hair as she peered into the mirror over my shoulder, "you had best decide quickly, for I have a feeling that our dear Mama will be very focused on the new batch of officers that will be arriving to join the militia... and if you should hope to avoid the life of a soldier's wife—"

I pushed her away gently and Jane laughed.

"Oh, hush," I grumbled, "you must not tease me about such things."

"Then there will be nothing left for me to tease you about," she said with a smile. "You are quite perfect otherwise."

"You are very funny," I grumbled as I pinned my hair up for the day ahead.

"Come along," Jane said. "We must wake the girls. Mama will be coming down for tea soon enough."

I took one last look in the mirror before I slid another pin into my curls and turned to follow my sister.

"I am already awake and dressed, you needn't knock on my door," Mary said from the corridor.

I took a deep breath and stepped out of the room. Mary was already in a sour mood, something which Lydia would immediately remark upon. A wonderful start to the day.

Perhaps I should have stayed in bed.

Jane kissed Mary's cheek. "Go downstairs then. Mrs. Hill will have started breakfast. Papa will be in his study, see that he has his tea."

"I shall do that," I blurted out. I rushed past Jane and Mary and raced down the stairs to the main level of the house.

"Lizzy—" Jane's exasperation was clear, but I could not bear

Lydia's whining, nor Kitty's inevitable chatter about her impending marriage. There was time enough for that later.

I did not doubt that Mary was of a similar mind to me... she had shown no interest in the matchmaking games that our mother liked to play, and in turn, Mama had ignored Mary entirely when it came to suggesting potential matches for her oft forgotten middle daughter.

I smiled as I reached the door of Papa's study. I tapped lightly upon it and then entered the room. It was a familiar place, one full of fond memories of reading by the fire, and tracing the outline of maps with my finger while he told me about the countries that lay beyond England's green shores.

"Why, Lizzy, it is you," my father said. He was seated behind his desk, as usual, his ledgers open before him and his favorite quill set into an ink well. "What is it that brings you here so early in the morning?"

I turned to him with a smile. "You must forgive me, Papa. I did not mean to disturb you. I was simply trying to avoid Mama's schemes."

"You are too late," he said as he turned his face away from me and pretended to return to his book. "I have been expecting her to burst in here any minute now. If she finds that you have escaped her plotting, she might believe that I was involved in some way..."

I laughed. "And what would be her reaction?"

"She would most likely say that I was no better than my brother," he replied. He glanced up at me and smiled. "But she would not be entirely wrong, now would she?"

"No, indeed," I said with a smile.

"Your Mama believes me to be a very foolish man, willing to get into any scheme that she might devise... but after four-and-twenty years of marriage she has not yet convinced me into any."

It was difficult not to laugh and the twinkle in my father's eye made it even more so.

"It vexes me deeply, Lizzy, and I am not afraid to say so. I will not have your mother's scheming ruin your chances of making a good match. Or Jane. Nothing would please me more than to see you both happily married before I die—"

"Papa—"

"And nothing would vex me more than to see you married to some half-wit your mother has chosen on a whim— it is fortunate that young Mr. Mason has some prospects to provide for Kitty, otherwise I would have turned him away in a trice!"

I could not stop my laughter this time. Papa's indignant tone was more than I could bear.

"You laugh," he huffed. "But think of my own suffering as I am to bear the brunt of Mrs. Bennet's machinations!"

"My poor Papa," I soothed. "Shall I call for some tea and biscuits?"

"Yes, indeed," he grumped.

I wanted to tell him then that I did not plan to marry, but I knew that such a pronouncement would weigh heavily upon him. We all knew that Mr. Collins' claim to Longbourn hovered at the edge of the horizon.

When Papa died, the estate would pass to him as Papa's only living male relative. He would, of course, wish for all of us to be married and well taken care of—and by extension that Mama would be taken care of as well.

I could hear my sisters' footsteps as they descended the stairs and I was reminded that any solace I could find in the early hours of the morning was fleeting.

"I shall bring you some tea," I said with a smile. "And I shall keep Mama from pestering you for as long as I am able."

"See that you do," my father said with a smile as he focused on his ledgers once more.

Two

"**M**ust you really go to London now?"

My mother was seated in her chair with her feet upon the ottoman that Mrs. Hill had dragged over to her. My mother's nerves, as ever, dictated the momentum of the household, and today she was not leaving her bedchamber or the comfortable chair that usually held her sewing box.

The Meryton Assembly was only a few weeks away, and there was a good deal of preparation still to be done.

My younger sisters were currently arguing over who would be wearing the dark blue satin gown that my mother had ordered from London—it had been meant for Jane, but now that Kitty was engaged, it seemed only right that she should wear it. But Lydia would not hear of it and their arguments went long into the night. I feared that someone would have to step in and declare that no one could wear the dress, but there had been no indication of where our mother's inclination lay... not yet in any case.

Jane and I had already ordered new ribbons for my gown from the dressmaker in Meryton. Although I had no need for such fripperies, I did feel a certain amount of anticipation for the approach of the annual event.

Although Meryton was a small town and the Assembly was rarely exciting, that did not mean that I couldn't enjoy the distraction of the dances and the chance to overhear some of the gossip that my dear friend Charlotte had collected from her mother's parlor.

But right now, all I wished for was to leave Hertfordshire and lose myself in the business of London.

Where no one had heard that Mrs. Eugenia Bennet was desperate to find husbands for her four daughters.

"But Lizzy, what about Jane's ribbons?" my mother asked desperately. "Should you not at least remain here long enough to be certain that they are delivered?"

"They are just ribbons, Mama," I said with a sigh. "There is no reason that Mrs. Cresswell will not have them here in plenty of time. You do not need me to oversee such a thing."

My mother's lips pressed into a thin line and I knew that she was trying to think of some reason that I should stay...

"Mama, I really must reply to my aunt," I said. "She is expecting me, and I would not wish to disappoint her."

"No, no," she sighed. "I suppose not. Heaven forbid that you disappoint your dear aunt at the same time as your dear Mama!"

I rolled my eyes toward the ceiling and bit down hard on my cheek. I could never say what was really on my mind. Not here. I knew that my mother only wished for the best for us, but sometimes it was difficult to see it.

"I shall only be gone for a fortnight," I said with a warm smile. "And the ball will be held on Saturday—three full weeks away. Surely you will not miss me that much?"

"I suppose not," she said, but I could see the lines around her mouth and I knew that she was disappointed.

"It has been fully agreed that I shall stay with Aunt Gardiner and be properly chaperoned," I said, hoping to make her feel better.

"Yes, well," my mother said, although she still did not look convinced.

"I thought you would be happy that I would be going to London," I said. "You have always said that the possibility of meeting a potential suitor is much greater in the city than it would be here in Hertfordshire."

A familiar light glinted in my mother's eyes. I had said the magical words.

Potential suitor.

"Oh, I am," she agreed. "It is just that I shall be worried about you, Lizzy. I do not think this is the right time to leave, not when your sisters are all at such delicate... positions." She dabbed at her eyes with her lace-edged handkerchief. The one she used when she was, very obviously, not in distress. "It is more important than ever that we find husbands for you and Jane before you become too old to be of interest."

"Mama—"

My mother held up her hand. "Now, I will not hear any argument. Lady Lucas has given upon her poor Charlotte. She is six and twenty! And still without a suitor! That could be Jane! That could be you!"

"Just promise that when you are in London that you will entertain every opportunity to find a match," my mother continued. "I shall write to Mrs. Gardiner and tell her of our plight so that she might assist us..."

"Indeed," I muttered and then swallowed hard, hoping that my mother had not heard me.

But she was not listening. She had turned her attention back to the letters upon her tea tray.

"And I believe that I shall send a letter to Mrs. Naughton as well... I shall ask her to call upon any of her sons that may be in the city and see if any of them are in want of a wife. I am sure that she knows much about the business of finding husbands, having been married four times herself..."

"Yes, Mama," I sighed.

I had been developing a plan in the last few weeks... one that would see an end to all of this nonsense.

It was almost foolproof.

Almost.

All I needed to do was leave Hertfordshire and allow my aunt, and gossip, to do the rest.

I did not have a suitor... but by the time I arrived in London, I would have one. He did not have to be real, he only needed to be believable.

My mother's pride would do the rest.

"I shall go and pack my valise," I said, interrupting my mother's muttering. "I shall be leaving for London in the morning."

"Yes, yes," Mama said absently.

I turned away from her and left the room, closing the door behind me as I made my way down the corridor toward the chamber I shared with Jane.

It was time to put my plan into action.

I had thought it over carefully, and I was determined to see it through.

But who would I choose to be my suitor?

I had spent the last few months watching the men in Hertfordshire and had finally settled upon one sort of gentleman. One who would be excellent company, and who would not be troubled to have a wife with a strong opinion on many matters...

A solicitor he must be.

Someone calm and measured, but with a strong aptitude for argument.

Handsome, surely, and with a goodly sense of humor.

Dark hair. Dark eyes... and a good deal taller than myself, which was not difficult to achieve.

Most importantly, he would have business that kept him in London or Bath for long periods of time, and perhaps clients who would keep him overseas for extended stays at their chateaux and villas.

Yes.

As much time apart as possible, but a connection that would inspire a companionship that neither of us could live without.

Such a gentleman did not exist—at least he did not exist in Hertfordshire. Perhaps not anywhere.

So much the better.

I was fully prepared to write letters to myself in said gentleman's hand and carry the ruse along until Jane had found her own husband... and when she did, my real aims could be fulfilled.

Marriage, or any semblance of it, did not factor into those aims.

I would only marry for the very deepest love... and that was something that I had begun to believe did not exist at all.

Therefore it seemed practical to choose an equally impossible gentleman. If I played my cards correctly, my mother would have no choice but to leave me alone. She would be content with the distraction of a suitor, and frustrated by any attempts to learn more about him. She would be so focused upon her fruitless search for answers that I would be free to assist Jane in her own search for a husband, and Kitty with the preparations for her wedding.

I packed my valise with a smile upon my face. It pained me that I would have to keep the truth from my dear aunt, but though I wished that I could bring her into my ruse, she would never agree to such a thing.

As much as she loved me, Mrs. Gardiner was as invested in my finding a suitable husband as my mother should have been.

Where my mother seemed only to be concerned with finding a warm body to occupy the position of 'husband,' my aunt wished for me to be *happy*.

But her version of my happiness also came at the cost of my own freedom, and I could not abide that.

~

L ondon in autumn was not an ideal time... the leaves on the trees in the various parks that were scattered throughout the city were, of course, beautiful. But it was nothing to Hertfordshire's rolling hills and thick copses of oak and birch trees that changed color all at once with the turn of the season.

And it rained. The fog off the Thames was thick and pungent at this time of year, and it would be a lie to say that I was looking forward to spending time in the city... but I was, very sincerely, excited to see my aunt and uncle. The Gardiners were a wonderful couple, and even if I was not related to them by blood, I would have endeavored to be close to them in friendship if I could.

My aunt and uncle were an example of how I believed a marriage should work. They appeared to truly enjoy the company of the other, and there was no vexatious talk or attempts to undermine as I so often observed in my own parents.

If I were to be married, I would wish for a partnership like the one that was shared in this household. I would often catch my aunt blushing as my uncle teased her, and the way her voice changed when she spoke of him, as though they were still courting... It was romantic and sweet. Even after so many years together, they were still as in love with each other as they had been on the day they were married.

Perhaps even more.

That was what I wished for.

But I could not dwell upon such a thing.

I had come to London to put a plan into motion.

One that would see my life as I would have it—without the involvement and pressure of a husband beating down upon me.

I would have my freedom.

I would have my independence.

If I could keep my nerve, this plan could give me time—perhaps even time enough for Jane to find a husband.

My aunt and uncle were waiting for me at the house on Gracechurch Street, and as the carriage approached, the sight of my aunt's smiling face warmed my heart. It would be good to be around family that was not distracted by a thousand different things all at once. The Gardiner household was a calm one, and I was desperately in need of some calm. If only for a short while.

Three

On a rare day when the rain had stopped, my aunt and I walked through St. James' Park to take in the changing autumn leaves and the business of the city. It was a wonderful thing to be among the rush of humanity that came with the city... My aunt did not seem bothered by any of it, but I found myself on the edge of being overwhelmed by all of the people, and the feel of their stares as we walked through the park.

"You must tell me everything, Lizzy," Mrs. Gardiner breathed. "Tell me all about Mr. Felix Drummond."

It sounded strange to hear my aunt say the name that I had plucked out of the air aloud. It did not make him real, but it... well, it almost did.

"I do not know what to tell you," I said. "Or where to begin!"

"How did you meet," she asked at once.

"It was... well, I am afraid that is not very exciting at all."

"A ball then... or a salon? Do not tell me that your Mama had finally found a match who was actually suitable for you!"

I laughed and gripped my aunt's arm tighter for just a moment. "No, indeed," I said. "It was very much by accident while I was visiting a friend in Hunsford—"

"Hunsford," Mrs. Gardiner exclaimed. "But how wonderful, that is a very wealthy area, is it not?"

"It may be," I said. I had only been to Hunsford once, and for a decidedly less pleasant reason. Visiting Mr. Collins at the parsonage had been one of the most tedious and terrible experiences of my life, eclipsed only by the terrible meeting with Lady Catherine de Bourgh which had accompanied it.

I wanted no part of what Mr. Collins had to offer, which was the only reason why my mother had put her plans to have us all married and 'well looked after' in the most efficient manner possible.

"And how, pray tell, did it happen?" Mrs. Gardiner pressed.

My smile was brief. "I was out walking, it was a beautiful summer afternoon, and he rode by on his horse—he stopped to ask for directions, and I had to admit that I did not know where I was..."

"A humorous beginning," my aunt said.

"It was," I agreed as I imagined the false scenario.

"Love at first sight," Mrs. Gardiner said with a sigh. "I recall the feeling well. I felt the same for your uncle— So many years ago now, but it seems like just yesterday I found him fishing by the river..." She smiled and shook off the memory. "But you have not described him to me!"

I had not. I had only a vague idea of what this impossible gentleman looked like, so I cast my gaze over the people who walked and rode through the park and settled upon a tall gentleman with dark hair that curled over his collar.

"Ah," I said. "I do apologize." I glanced at the gentleman once more, intent on describing him as accurately as possible. "He is tall, a little taller than Mr. Gardiner. He has dark hair, like mahogany, with a curl to it—"

"Ah," Mrs. Gardiner exclaimed. "Your children will have the most luscious curly hair!"

I laughed. "You cannot be planning for my children already," I protested.

"I would love them as my own children," my aunt promised. "And you must promise to bring them to Gracechurch Street as often as you can— Will you live in London after you are married?"

I let out a heavy sigh. "I could not say."

"And what else," Mrs. Gardiner pressed.

"His eyes are dark, and very intense. He is a serious gentleman, but with a softer side and a fondness for wild creatures. He has a wonderful laugh..."

"Delightful. Your uncle will offer to take him fishing, you must tell him."

"I shall," I promised.

"And what else? What does he do?"

"Do?"

Mrs. Gardiner pushed at me gently. "Do not be obtuse! What is his profession, Lizzy?"

I laughed and leaned against her shoulder as I stole one more glance at the gentleman on whom I had based Mr. Felix Drummond. He *was* handsome enough to be the sort of gentleman I might marry. He was with a beautiful young woman who laughed at the antics of the ducks upon the pond before them. He appeared unmoved, but then he surprised me as he smiled indulgently at the young woman as she threw bread into the water for the birds.

"He is a solicitor," I said. "Highly sought after. His clients keep him very busy— and he is often away from London."

"Well, that is not ideal at all," Mrs. Gardiner said. "Where will you settle after the wedding?"

"That is the trouble," I replied. "I do not know what might happen. He has made an offer of marriage, and I have accepted, but the rest—"

"Lizzy, but those are the most important details!"

"For now, it suits me very well," I said. "He writes very often, and has already sent several letters—"

Mrs. Gardiner sighed. "I suppose that will have to do for now... but I do hope that Mr—"

"Drummond," I said. "Felix Drummond."

"Mr. Drummond," she repeated. "I do hope that he will promise to find some sort of balance—it would not do to raise the children—"

"Children again," I chuckled. "Perhaps you might allow me to be married first before such conversations are undertaken?"

Mrs. Gardiner laughed. "Indeed, I shall endeavor to restrain my enthusiasm. But, Lizzie, I am ever so thrilled that you have found someone who suits your temperament. I did worry—"

"That I would not meet anyone at all?"

She made a face. "I did not say that. I only wish for your happiness, my dear."

"And I am grateful for it," I said with a smile as we walked on through the park. "But I can assure you that I have found it. The one thing I have been searching for in a partner is someone who sees me for who I really am and not a gentleman in search of a pretty bird to keep caged in the parlor to sing and preen when guests come to visit."

The lie tumbled from my lips with ease, as though it were natural and real.

My aunt's smile was jubilant. "I must say I cannot agree more. I cannot tell you how many gentlemen I turned aside who were seeking just such an ornament for a bride. I thought that I should have given up entirely before I met your uncle!" She laughed brightly. "But Lizzy, I cannot understand why your mother did not tell me about it sooner," she exclaimed. "She wrote at once when Kitty's engagement to Mr. Mason was made..."

"I daresay she would have written to you *before* it had been agreed if she had the opportunity," I said.

"That *is* possible," she laughed. "Oh, Lizzy, I am so happy for you!"

The truth lingered in my mind. A heavy burden.

I wanted to tell her that it was all a ruse. But it had happened so quickly, and the lie had felt so natural.

It would be easy to keep it up.

I could do this.

But not without Jane's help.

When I returned to Hertfordshire, preparations were well underway for the Netherfield Ball, and my aunt had decided that she would make the journey back to Meryton with me as Mr. Gardiner would be out of London on business with one of his warehouse investors.

"I would much rather be with family during this happy time," she said as the carriage rolled away toward Hertfordshire. "Your Mama will certainly need all of my assistance at this time. Two daughters engaged, and perhaps we might expect Jane to be in a similar situation soon enough!"

"We can only hope," I replied. I knew that I would have to do my best to tell Jane what was happening before my aunt could do so. Mama would, if my suspicions were correct, pretend that she had known all along and the younger girls would follow our mother's example.

"But Lizzy, there is something I must ask you—"

She did not give me the opportunity to answer before she continued. "How did you know?"

"Know what?" I replied, keeping my tone as light as possible.

"That Mr. Drummond was the one for you," she said. Her voice was light, chiding, yet it sent a chill down my spine.

"Oh," I said with a small smile. "I suppose I ... It was simply a feeling. You know me well enough to understand, surely?"

"Yes, of course," she said but her gaze was thoughtful. "A feeling, yes— It is certainly how it happened for me when I met your uncle." She smiled. "I suppose I should be grateful that one of my beloved nieces has found this kind of happiness."

"But," she continued, "I could not help but notice there are some details which are a little... lacking."

I looked away from her, staring out at the passing trees and fields as we drew nearer Hertfordshire and the rest of my family. The carriage hit a small hole in the road, and I bit back a gasp.

"I do not mean to question you, my dear," Mrs. Gardiner said, quickly. "I only thought that perhaps I should know a little more about my future nephew—"

"What else shall I tell you?" I asked brightly.

"You promised you would tell me of his background, perhaps that would be best," she said. "Do you know much about his family?"

"Only that he was raised by his father," I replied, struggling to remember what I had written in the letter. "He lost his mother when he was quite young, but I did not ask him to share any painful memories of her. I think he sees her as a figure to whom he must apologize for not being a better son."

"He sounds a little melancholy," Mrs. Gardiner said.

"I promise you that he is not," I replied. "He is very kind and has a great love for his father and his sisters."

"Very charming, indeed," she said. "And what do you know of his business?"

"As I mentioned before, I only know that he often goes out of London at the request of his clients quite often," I said.

"A goodly amount of time it seems," Mrs. Gardiner said. "Is that the kind of life you should wish to have, dearest? It will be terribly lonely for you if you do not accompany him."

I smiled at my aunt, for I had thought of a response for this, as well. "This is why we shall delay our marriage... Only for a short while, while he prepares his clients to be less in need of his personal attention. When he is established in London with local clients then we may be settled there."

Mrs. Gardiner seemed to accept this as a very reasonable answer. "A responsible choice," she said. "But he does have an income?"

"He does, indeed," I said. "At least four thousand a year."

"That much?" my aunt gasped.

I regretted that number instantly, but I wished for nothing more than this conversation to end. "He has a goodly list of clients who retain his services," I explained, "and his father died very recently and left him a tidy inheritance."

She nodded. "I suppose there is nothing more to ask—"

"I shall enquire after more details in my next letter," I promised. "I am desperately curious about his sisters."

Mrs. Gardiner smiled at me. "I am sure that your Mama will have plenty to say on the matter as well. I do so look forward to hearing more about Kitty's Mr. Mason as well!"

"Mama will have a good deal to say about him," I said with a smile. "He is a gentle young man and very well suited to Kitty, I think."

"Delightful," Mrs. Gardiner said with clear warmth. "I am so very pleased that Kitty was able to forgo some of her shyness to meet such a young man."

"I believe there was an equal amount of shyness and accident in their meeting," I laughed. "But you shall see for yourself at the assembly. Though I will warn you, Lydia has taken it upon herself to flirt with Mr. Mason at every opportunity—"

My aunt stared at me in surprise. "But— Why? Was Mr. Mason previously interested in courting Lydia?"

"Oh, no, indeed not," I said. "But as soon as Lydia learned of Kitty's affection for him she immediately turned her eye toward him. Thankfully, the gentleman is too clever to be taken in by her flirtations."

"Oh, but poor Kitty—"

"Indeed," I said with a sigh. "I can only hope that she will lose interest in a short amount of time. But there is a new cadre of officers coming to the garrison in a very short time and I daresay she will be properly distracted by the time the assembly arrives."

"Let us hope so," Mrs. Gardiner agreed. "That girl will find herself in more trouble than she is quite capable of handling if she is not careful..."

I looked out the carriage window to watch the countryside as we passed by. The cityscape had given way to dirt roads and wide estates with rolling green hills and placid cows... soon enough we would be back in Hertfordshire and I would have to work swiftly to bring Jane into my confidence. Mama and Mrs. Gardiner would keep themselves busy with their gossip, and my father would keep to his study as he always did during the preparations for the assembly.

I envied him more this year than I usually did.

Four

"Lizzy, you cannot be serious." Jane's voice cracked as she stared at me in disbelief. I rushed forward to cover her mouth with my hand, but she pushed me away.

"Please, do keep your voice down," I begged her. "No one must know—"

"Indeed, it would seem that way," Jane choked out. "Lizzy— Do you know what you have done?"

"Yes," I said firmly. "I have lied to our aunt, to our mother, to our sisters..."

"The whole of Meryton will know about this in a very short amount of time," Jane exclaimed.

"*Please*, keep your voice down," I begged again. It was a mercy that we were in the garden, but there was no telling who might overhear us. As much as Mrs. Hill loved us, her loyalty was to Mama first, and she would have no qualms about taking such information straight to her mistress without delay.

"But why did you do it," Jane protested.

"Why? I thought that would be obvious," I replied. "I do not wish to marry. I have always said that I would never be persuaded to do so except in the case that I stumbled upon the very deepest love. But, Jane, I do not believe that such a thing exists..."

"Lizzy—"

"Jane... it's the only way that I shall be able to fulfill my promise to you. You will find a wonderful husband, and I shall follow you to care for your children. Or would you rather see me unhappily married to someone of Mama's choosing? I have heard her say on more than one occasion that she would see me married to the very next gentleman who expressed an interest in making his suit—"

"Papa would never allow such a thing," Jane gasped.

I let out a heavy sigh. "I thought such a thing myself, for far too long... For far too long I believed that it would be so. But Mr. Collins— If something were to happen to Papa—"

"Lizzy, you must not speak such things," Jane hissed.

"But it is true," I said. "If something should happen to Papa, then we are, all of us, suddenly Mr. Collins' responsibility. Do you really believe that he will be so generous as to allow us to stay at Longbourn?"

"I—" Jane's shoulders slumped. "I must admit that I have pondered the very same thing."

"And there is nothing we can do about it," I said. "Except to—"

"To marry," Jane finished. "I know, Lizzy. But this... This is far too drastic!"

"Nonsense," I said. "I have everything well in hand."

Confidence was the only way that I would get through this.

"Do you, indeed?"

I nodded. "My dear Mr. Felix Drummond will write me letters every few weeks, each one giving some excuse or other as to why we cannot see each other, but that he sends all of his affection and well-wishes for the health of my dear parents and beloved sisters."

Jane shook her head, but there was a smile upon her face.

"Will you help me?" I asked.

Jane groaned aloud and looked up at the overcast sky. "Lizzy... I suppose that I have no choice..."

"Of course you have a choice," I said. "You may, of course, tell Mama that it is all a farce and that I am lying in order to avoid being forced to marry a gentleman that I cannot tolerate, or, even worse, Mr. Collins, in an effort to rescue us from being cast out of the home we have spent our entire lives in."

"Lizzy, this is not a game," Jane said softly.

"Of course it is not," I agreed. "It does not matter whether or not you choose to help me. Either way, I will carry out my scheme. But it so happens that, quite frankly, I would rather not be alone in this."

Jane frowned. "So you have decided to put more pressure upon my shoulders to find a good match before Mama becomes suspicious of the fact that Mr. Felix Drummond is never available to visit or escort you to a ball?"

"Perhaps," I said.

A long pause hung between us and I thought for certain that she would not agree... but then Jane slowly nodded her head.

"Very well. But if I am to do this properly, and be your witness to your first meeting with this imaginary gentleman, you must allow me to read all of these letters you have created."

I smiled at my sister and wrapped my arm around her waist to pull her against my side. "I shall do that at once. Come— we have much to talk about."

～

The most difficult part of this scheme was to be certain that my mother did not become suspicious. As I had hoped, when my aunt mentioned the engagement to congratulate her on another daughter's impending nuptials, Mama pretended that she already knew what had occurred.

"I recall it very well," she said proudly. "I have never seen my Lizzy so captivated by a gentleman."

"Indeed it would seem that Mr. Drummond is very fortunate, indeed," Mrs. Gardiner said with a smile.

"I know my Lizzy," my mother said. "She has made a very good match, and we are all *very* proud of her. Now, the mystery remains as to when the wedding will take place. We cannot allow it to overshadow Kitty's wonderful day."

"No, indeed," I said. I had no plans to overshadow anything at all. "Mr. Drummond—Felix—will be away from London on business for some time. But I am expecting a letter very soon that will tell me how long he intends to be away."

"Always so busy," Mama said with a sigh. "I do hope that he will have some time to keep a wife."

"That is the plan, Mama," I said. "As soon as he is able to maintain a steady income and household in London, then we shall move forward with our plans."

"Wonderful," Mrs. Gardiner said.

"Kitty's wedding shall be just after Christmastide," Mrs. Bennet announced. "So we shall have to hope that Mr. Drummond might be persuaded to make good on his promises so that Lizzy might be a spring bride. Would that not be a wonderful thing?"

"Indeed, it would."

I could say nothing. I could only look into my teacup and smile as though nothing in the world would make me happier.

Lying was very difficult, but I had to console myself with the fact that I had done everything in my power to make her understand that I did not wish to marry. But she had not listened, and so I had been driven to this. But it was not my mother that I was doing this for, was it? I was doing it for my sisters, for our future.

Ultimately, I was doing this for Jane.

As I had said to Jane, I did not believe in true love... or the love that I had pined for since I was very young. I did not even believe that I would fall in love—which was, perhaps, why this fiction was so easy to fall into. It was easy to pretend that something I had always hoped for was real. But deep down I did not believe that I would have a family of my own. Jane's family would have to be enough for me.

And it would be. I was certain of that.

The Meryton assembly approached with an uncomfortable swiftness and I did my best to keep up my fiction with Jane's reluctant assistance. She agreed with everything that I said about Mr. Drummond, and offered her own version of how we had met that was far more endearing than the one I told—a fact that she explained at my modesty about how charming and heartwarming it had all been.

There were no words for how grateful I was for her support, especially when rumors of my engagement began to be spoken of in Meryton. Soon enough, as Jane had warned me, everyone knew something of it—they knew the gentleman's occupation, and what he looked like... They even knew that he had been raised by his father. As soon as Mama had taken tea with Lady Lucas, it was certain that the news of the engagement would spread, but I had not been prepared for the speed of it.

But, when the flurry of interest died down, so did any other talk of potential suitors. And in even less time, my mother's focus once again turned to Kitty and Mr. Mason—a vastly preferable topic as Mr. Mason was in Meryton and could be called upon for dinner engagements and visits for tea.

As soon as it had begun, the excitement and interest in my new engagement was forgotten. Every so often, Mama would ask to see Mr. Drummond's latest letter, which I would dutifully produce so that she could exclaim over the grace of his penmanship and the flourish in the initials he always signed his letters with.

"Ever your servant, F. D."

She would read the words I had written aloud to my sisters and sigh happily as they imagined what her newly acquired son-in-law would look like and sound like when he was paying her a compliment or enquiring after her health.

But then I would be forgotten again.

With the Meryton assembly only days away, the focus of the household was on preparations for the much anticipated event. The last assembly before Christmastide was always a mad rush for every young lady in Meryton. New officers would arrive in town just in time to make an appearance at the assembly in their fine red jackets and highly polished boots, and there were always far too many young ladies and never enough gentlemen to partner with them.

But now I did not have to worry about such things.

Mama would not expect me to be seen with a new partner for every dance, and I could spend my time speaking to my dear friend Charlotte. Or perhaps I would keep a watchful eye upon Lydia, which seemed all the more important seeing as Kitty was freshly engaged and Lydia was in search of a foolproof way to steal back some of the attention she had lost.

But before the assembly, I had to speak to my father.

As I had hoped, my father had stayed sequestered in his study since my aunt's arrival. It was not that he disliked Mrs. Gardiner, it was only that he was dreadfully outnumbered and the house had taken on a certain level of noise that always accompanied the approach of any major social event.

The study was his only refuge. My mother knew better than to disturb him, and I was the only one who was permitted to enter.

He answered my knock immediately and I entered the room with a smile upon my face.

I was not surprised to find him seated at his desk, poring over his ledgers and paperwork. Papa was always happiest when he was busily working on something, and the small estate that surrounded Longbourn seemed to keep him quite occupied.

Even though I did not like to think about it, I imagined that he was making certain that everything was in order for when Mr. Collins would take over ownership... but I could not bring myself to talk to him about that.

"Lizzy!" He put down his quill with a smile. "Has your mother driven you mad with talk about the assembly yet? I had hoped that your aunt's arrival would calm her nerves somewhat... but it seems that the noise in the house has only increased since your return from London."

"There is a good reason for that, Papa," I replied.

His thick eyebrows rose. "Oh?"

"I had hoped to speak with you about it. Are you busy?"

"I am never too busy for you, my dear. But I have a feeling from the look on your face that I might require a cup of tea to accompany this news."

A pot of tea and a plate of biscuits had been brought in earlier, and I was pleased to find that it was still warm.

"So what is this news that you must speak to me about?" He asked as I poured two cups and prepared my father's the way he liked it.

"It is a very happy matter," I said brightly. "Very happy, indeed."

"Indeed?"

I set the cup down upon his desk and sank down into the chair across from him.

"If you are here to speak to me about Kitty's wedding gown, you may tell your mother that I will not pay for the lace that she wishes to order from Paris. It is ridiculous. She may take her complaints to Mr. Mason—"

"No, Papa," I laughed. "It is not about French lace."

"Then what is it?"

I took a deep breath. "I am engaged to be married."

He set his cup down with a crash and I flinched.

"What—"

"Papa—"

"You did not ask for my opinion on the gentleman? You did not think to ask what I might have to say on the matter?"

"Papa— if you will allow me—"

"And who is he? Who is this gentleman? Is he even a gentleman at all that he did not come to visit me and speak to me in person? How could you even agree to such a thing! Lizzy!"

I set down my cup and folded my hands in my lap. My father's cheeks and ears were red—in truth I had never seen him so flustered.

"Papa. The gentleman in question does... Well, he does not exist."

"What!" My father's roar was loud and I winced as I hoped that mother had not heard it.

"Hush, Papa," I hissed. "I shall explain!"

"With haste," he said flatly.

I took a deep breath. "Papa, as you well know, Mama has been intent on making matches for all of her daughters so that we might be married as soon as possible..."

My father grumbled and crossed his arms over his chest.

"With the threat of Mr. Collins looming on the horizon, I fear that she has lost all reason when it comes to these matches... she has threatened to see me engaged to the next gentleman who expresses any interest in gaining a wife!"

"Lizzy— When it comes to Mr. Collins—"

"It is not your fault, Papa," I said quickly. "But Mama has been very insistent." I clasped my hands in my lap. "In order to avoid her machinations I *invented* a gentleman. I *invented* an engagement."

"But, Lizzy, why?"

I straightened my shoulders and met my father's gaze. "I do not wish to be married, Papa."

"Then what plans do you have, dearest? If you are not to marry—"

"I shall live with Jane," I said. "She will not be far away from an engagement of her own, and she will need my assistance to run her household and manage her children. I would much prefer that life than to be a wife to a gentleman I hardly know and cannot stand the sight of."

That seemed to calm his temper somewhat, and he uncrossed his arms and rested his elbows upon his desk.

"I see," he said. "And why would you tell me this?"

"I have brought Jane into my confidence," I said. "But I could not continue this ruse without your assistance."

"So... You are not engaged. Is that what you are saying?"

"I am not," I said and dared to smile. "This gentleman, he does not exist anywhere but within my mind, and within the false letters that I have written to prove his existence."

My father chuckled and shook his head. "I do believe this is the only way I would have approved of any engagement," he said. "And your mother? What was her reaction?"

"She was... very surprised, but hid it well and I believe she has convinced my aunt that she knew about the engagement all along."

My father laughed. "Bless your Mama for her pride," he muttered as he picked up his teacup once more. "And you say that this gentleman does not exist?"

"Certainly not, Papa," I replied.

"And what might be gained from bringing me into your confidence?"

"It is a... precaution," I said. "If Mama should happen to speak to you about it, I will need your assurance that you will be willing to—"

"To lie," my father said.

I nodded. "Yes."

He let out a heavy sigh and took a sip of his tea. "What is this fictional young man's name?"

"Oh, Papa," I exclaimed. I jumped up from my chair and rushed around the desk to press a kiss to his forehead.

"Now, now," he grumbled and I pulled away to resume my seat. "And what is it that I am supposed to say about this gentleman?"

"Only that you approve of the match," I said. "There is not much else to say. The gentleman I have invented spends much of his time working and away from London—he is a lawyer."

My father snorted. "A lawyer who would rather work than spend time with you? This fictional gentleman is a fool, Lizzy."

My smile broadened. "Indeed, he may well be."

"And how long do you plan to keep this fiction alive?"

"Until Jane has secured an engagement."

"And then what?"

I let out a dramatic sigh. "Then, I shall receive a letter that bears some terrible news—"

"Terrible?"

"Indeed," I said. "That my dear Mr. Drummond has had a change of heart, and that we may no longer be married. Or some such thing."

"How very upsetting," my father said. "I shall, of course, be angered beyond all reason to have my daughter slighted so. Mr. Drummond would not dare to show his face in Hertfordshire ever again."

"That is my hope," I said. "And I shall be too heartbroken to take any interest in marriage ever again."

My father chuckled and leaned back in his chair. "Your plan seems very thorough, Lizzy," he said.

I inclined my head at his compliment. "I do hope so."

"As do I," he said.

Five

In the days before the assembly, I could take some solace in the fact that my mother's attention was drawn in several different directions. But a new opportunity had also presented itself—one that my mother could not ignore.

"Mama will not stop talking about it," Jane said with a sigh.

We were seated in the parlor with our gowns for the assembly in our laps. Jane was busy adding to the whitework embroidery on the bodice of her gown, while I struggled to add a pale pink velvet ribbon to the sleeves of Kitty's ivory gown.

Kitty would ask for my assistance with every alteration of her gowns, and this one was no exception. She had complained bitterly that she had not been permitted to buy a new gown for the assembly, but there would be no arguments now that she was engaged—all of the focus was upon that day... and not on something as mundane as the Meryton assembly.

"I cannot blame her," I said with a smile. "And neither should you. You know she would be overjoyed if you were to catch the eye of a wealthy gentleman with five thousand a year—"

"Is it so much," she murmured.

"You know very well that it is," I laughed.

Jane frowned as she laid another stitch into her pattern. "And what if he does not dance with me? What if he does not come to the assembly at all?"

"Despite what Papa has said, he has, indeed, been to Netherfield Park to visit Mr. Bingley. He is only trying to vex our mother with his denials."

Jane let out a heavy sigh.

"You have nothing to be worried about," I said with confidence. "This gentleman would be a fool to ignore you."

"There are a great many young ladies in Hertfordshire—" Jane began.

"And none as beautiful, or as kind and wonderful as you," I said firmly. "The assembly will be a triumph, I have no fear of that, and you should not either."

"It is only an assembly," Jane murmured, but her cheeks were flushed and there was a smile upon her face as she focused on her needlework once more.

"I daresay that Mr. Bingley will be certain to ask you to dance. And more than once..."

Jane laughed as I nudged her with my elbow. "You must stop teasing me," she protested, "you are making me lose my stitches!"

"Now if only Lydia would cease her endless teasing—poor Kitty must be tired of hearing how she has made her engagement too soon."

"Lydia will say anything to vex our sister," Jane sighed. "But surely Kitty must know that her match with Mr. Mason is a good one that will benefit us all..."

"She does," I said. "I have no doubt of that, but Lydia is... incorrigible."

"As ever." Jane pulled her needle away from her whitework and smiled. "And what of yourself, Lizzy? What are your plans for the assembly?"

"I have not decided," I said. "I do have a great deal to speak to Charlotte about..."

"I imagine that you shall not be subjected to Mama's endless parade of eligible bachelors. But that was your aim all along, was it not?"

I grinned at my sister. "Indeed it was. I shall pretend to be forlorn that I do not have a partner, but as Mr. Drummond is not overly fond of dancing, I would not have found myself on the dance floor more than once or twice if he were there."

"How very unfortunate, indeed," Jane said. "Perhaps he would be more fond of dancing if you taught him some of our 'quaint country dances.'"

"Perhaps when next I am able to see him," I laughed. "However, since he shall not be in attendance, I shall play my part until Mama loses interest, and then I shall recover and find Charlotte."

"She will be as full of gossip as her mother," Jane said with a smile. "And I do believe the most delicious gossip this season is your secret and very sudden engagement."

"Indeed, it may well be," I replied.

Voices in the corridor silenced our conversation and I turned my full attention back to the gown in my lap. I was nearly finished, and Kitty would need to try on the gown to be certain that everything was in place...

My fingers were cramped and I still had alterations to make to my own gown.

"Do you have Mr. Drummond's newest letter," Jane hissed.

"I do," I murmured as I pulled the letter from my ribbon basket and held it up. I had only written it the night before, and it contained all of the dear gentleman's heartfelt apologies for his absence and some talk of his travels in Paris and beyond.

"Mama will be asking for it," Jane whispered.

And, indeed, even before she had entered the parlor, our mother's voice carried into the room.

"Lizzy, have you had a letter from our dear Mr. Drummond? How I do long to see him and speak to him!"

My mother swept into the room with Kitty following close

behind her. When Kitty's engagement to Mr. Mason had been confirmed, she had usurped Lydia's position as our mother's favorite. It would not last very long, but I could not discourage her from enjoying the long overdue attention she now received.

"I do, Mama," I said. "Would you like to read it—"

"Is he coming to the assembly?"

I shook my head sadly. "No, Mama, I am afraid he is in Paris for the next several weeks—his clients keep him very busy."

I held out the letter and my mother snatched it from my fingers and opened it eagerly.

"Oh, Lizzy. I know I say this every time, but you really must insist that he come to Hertfordshire to visit. I am long overdue to welcome him to Longbourn—"

"Yes, Mama," I murmured. I knew she was not really listening to me. She did not wish to have my input. She wished only to speak her thoughts aloud with no care for what might happen when she had finished.

A conversation without consequence.

"He writes of Paris, Francis," she said to my aunt who entered the parlor and took a seat beside me upon the couch. Mrs. Gardiner's smile was warm as she examined my work on Kitty's gown.

"How wonderful," my aunt said. "I have not been to Paris since I was a young bride. I do hope that Mr. Drummond will take you to Paris after you are married, Lizzy."

"Perhaps," I replied.

"Perhaps!" My mother let out a small cry of indignation. "Indeed he *must*! I shall have your Papa demand that it be so."

My mother's outcry was all for her own benefit. I knew how much she would have wished to tell all of her friends that her daughter was to visit Paris after her marriage. *How wonderful. How extravagant.*

How tiresome all of this was.

If there was anything that might give me cause to reveal the truth of it all, it was the tediousness of this endless speculation and conversation.

My mother read the rest of the letter with eager eyes and touched upon all of the highlights that I supposed she would.

"He will be in Paris for several weeks," she exclaimed. "I do hope he will send you something for all the trouble he is putting you through. A gift as an apology for the strain on your nerves— Perhaps a new fan, or some silk—"

"A new fan," Kitty breathed. "All the way from Paris! No one in Hertfordshire will have one like that!"

"Of course they would not," Mama snapped. "No one in Hertfordshire would go to Paris. Even Lady Lucas would be hard pressed to make such a voyage." My mother glanced at me and smiled. "You should ask him to send you a fan, Lizzy. Something elegant and refined... A parasol, perhaps!"

"Of course, Mama," I said.

"It would be the height of rudeness to deny his future wife anything she might desire," my mother continued. "Why, if he does not comply, I shall have to write to him with some harsh words—"

My aunt's cough interrupted my mother's tirade. "Kitty, you should try on the gown that Lizzy has altered for you. I do believe you will look very well in it."

Kitty's cheeks flushed prettily as she approached to inspect the work I had done. The pale pink color of the velvet ribbons would look very nice under the candlelight, and I had enough to make something for her hair as well.

"You have done a lovely job," my aunt said as she pulled the gown from my lap and held it out to Kitty. "Here, my dear," she said to Kitty. "Go and put it on so that we might see how beautiful you will look."

"She will look like a potato covered in ribbons," Lydia grumbled.

"Lydia," Mama snapped. "You will cease to have an opinion at once."

Lydia's mouth dropped open in surprise. She had always been our mother's favorite and this change of attitude was most unexpected. Jane and I knew that it would fade as soon as Kitty became Mrs. Mason, but for now, Lydia would have to get used to a different hierarchy in the household.

Whether or not she would do as she was told remained to be seen.

Kitty gathered up the gown in her arms and rushed from the room. I busied myself with putting away my thread and scissors as Kitty's footsteps echoed above us.

My mother held out the letter and smiled in a self-satisfied way as she scanned Mr. Drummond's false words once more.

"Paris," she sighed. "Just think of it, Lizzy— But you do not seem excited at all!"

"I am, Mama," I said with a smile. "It is just...difficult to think of myself when we should all be focused on Kitty's approaching nuptials."

"Yes, yes," my mother huffed. She set down the letter and picked up her handkerchief, ready to dab at her eyes in a dramatic fashion when Kitty reappeared.

I did not relish the day when Kitty would be fitted for her wedding gown and we would have to bear Mama's histrionics afresh. I could feel that she was building toward it with every passing day, and when it finally arrived I did not know if I would be able to be present.

"Must she take so *long*," Lydia moaned. She draped herself over her chair and sighed heavily. "I am half-starved!"

"Hush," Mama snapped.

Kitty's footsteps echoed on the stairs as she ran back down to the main floor and along the corridor to the parlor.

There was a distinct flush to my younger sister's cheeks as she entered the room. "Well? What do you think?"

The gown had been altered no more shockingly than anything else I had done for her in the years before it—but for some reason she looked entirely different than any other year. Perhaps it was her impending marriage, or the fact that she was receiving positive attention for the first time in her life, but Kitty fairly glowed with barely contained joy and something else I could not place.

Was this what it would be like to be in love? Was my sister *truly* in love with this Mr. Mason?

Was this how I should act?

It was so difficult to know—and yet, I did not know if I could pretend to such affection. Mama would expect such a display from Kitty, which meant that I might be able to escape such embarrassment. But I would have to continue my small smiles (which I hoped contained a hint of sadness at Mr. Drummond's continued absence) and demure replies to my mother's incessant questions.

I would have to think about how much I was willing to put into this pantomime, and hope that it would not be drawn out too long—I did not wish to put pressure on Jane to find a husband, but there was only so much that I could bear.

Perhaps this gentleman at Netherfield Park would prove as interesting as Mama hoped.

～

M y own expectations for the assembly were not lofty. Every year the same amount of effort was put into the event by the ladies of the Hertfordshire Society, and each year Lady Lucas would take all responsibility for its success. Whether it was the decor, the refreshments, or the quality of the musicians, she would always find some way to take credit for everything that occurred that could garner some praise.

The assembly rooms themselves were in dire need of refurbishment, but the swags of velvet and damask material that had been hung from the beams did a great deal to disguise some of its shabbiness.

Under the soft glow of candlelight, there were many things that could be overlooked and forgiven.

I had no expectation of anything other than the usual tedium that accompanied the event. Kitty and Lydia were excited for anything that would allow them to dance and show off, but Kitty's enthusiasm was now tempered by the fact that she would be on display as a newly engaged woman, not just a silly girl who giggled too much and laughed when she did not know what to say.

Engagement to Mr. Mason had brought about a positive change in Kitty, and I did truly hope that she would find some happiness with the young man.

When Jane and I arrived with Mrs. Gardiner, the room was already full of people and the dancing was already in full swing. Kitty was seated on a chair near the edge of the dance floor while Lydia spun on the arm of one of her favorite officers.

Kitty's gaze was fixed on the door and she smiled as I approached. As was usual, there were too many young ladies in Hertfordshire, which meant that there were never enough partners to go around. Much of the evening would be spent seated in the chairs that had been set out as we waited for our turn upon the dance floor.

I sat down on the chair beside Kitty and patted her hand. "Has Mr. Mason not arrived yet?"

Kitty shook her head. "No. Hopefully he will be along soon. I am so eager to see him, and I do not wish to be away from the dance floor for too long! Lydia has already taken two partners!"

I glanced at the dance floor and frowned at my younger sister. Lydia was a selfish creature, but she was young, and I could not fault her for everything. She thought of nothing and no one but herself and her own pleasure—a fault that was surely more to do with my mother's doting affection than anything.

Mrs. Gardiner approached us and held out a glass of punch which I took with a grateful smile. "I am pleased to see you waiting, Kitty," she said. "Now that you are engaged, your first dance must be with Mr. Mason. You should not be seen dancing with too many partners. Especially before his arrival."

Kitty's lips pursed and she nodded. "Yes, I know, Aunt." Kitty's dutiful reply was rewarded with a kiss upon her cheek.

"Thank you, my darling," Mrs. Gardiner said.

"Have the occupants of Netherfield Park arrived yet?" I asked Kitty.

My sister nodded and pointed to the opposite side of the room. "There are three gentlemen and two ladies," she said.

Mrs. Gardiner looked in the direction that Kitty had indicated and her eyes narrowed. "Lizzy— could you describe Mr. Drummond for me, I seem to have forgotten."

My aunt's question took me by surprise and I tried to recall the gentleman I had seen in London. "I— He has dark hair, long enough to curl over the collar of his jacket, fine dark eyes..."

"He is of a goodly height is he not?" she asked. "With a stern countenance and a serious look to him—"

"Why, yes, you have remembered him very well," I said.

"Lizzy," she said in a hushed voice. "He is here."

I stood up in alarm and my aunt grabbed my arm. "There," she hissed. "Standing near the party from Netherfield Park—that is him. Exactly as you described him. I would swear it was."

My eyes swept over the crowd and settled upon the gentleman she had indicated. My throat tightened as I looked at him. It was, indeed, the gentleman from the park. The very one who had become the model for my fictional future husband.

"Oh, I am certain you are mistaken," I murmured.

"He looks very much as you described," my aunt said. "The hair, the intensity of his gaze... Oh, Lizzy—"

I shook my head. "Impossible," I said with a smile. "You know as well as I do that Mr. Drummond is in Paris for the next fortnight, perhaps longer. He would not come here without telling me—"

My aunt's forehead creased. "You are quite correct, Lizzy," she said. "I merely hoped that he might be here to surprise you. But, alas, these are the fantasies of a hopelessly romantic woman who would wish to see all of her nieces happily married."

She pulled me against her side. "I shall go and speak to your mother, she is embroiled in conversation with Lady Lucas, and I do not wish to miss any of the gossip from Hertfordshire."

"Indeed," I murmured. I forced myself to smile as my aunt moved away through the crowd, but I could not take my eyes off the dark-haired gentleman on the opposite side of the room.

Who was he and what was he doing in Hertfordshire?

Six

I spent the entirety of the evening distracted and frantic that my aunt would mention something to my mother about the mystery gentleman who looked so very much like the gentleman I had created.

Charlotte was able to answer some of my questions. Lady Lucas made it her business to know everything that happened in Hertfordshire, especially when it came to new faces in town.

Thankfully, all eyes were upon Jane and the gentleman who had leased Netherfield Park. Mr. Charles Bingley had sought my sister out almost immediately as his dance partner, and they had taken more than three dances together during the evening. The stern gentleman who had accompanied him, as Charlotte informed me, was Mr. Fitzwilliam Darcy. A somewhat more mysterious figure than Mr. Bingley.

He did not dance with anyone, and seemed to prefer to stand to the side and watch the activity in the room.

"The two ladies are Mr. Bingley's sisters," Charlotte informed me. "Mama tells me that they are very refined, indeed, and very accomplished. Their gowns are the height of London fashion—"

"Which explains why they look so out of place here," I

murmured. "Every young lady in Hertfordshire will stampede to the dress shop to order dyed ostrich feathers..."

Charlotte snorted into her cup of punch. "I do not doubt it. We have been so starved for any kind of fashion that it would be a welcome change."

"Perhaps," I mused.

What I truly wished was to know more about the dark-eyed gentleman. He was, indeed, stern, and he seemed not to smile at all through the course of the evening. He spoke to no one but Mr. Bingley and his sisters, and the third gentleman who had come with them seemed to do nothing more but drink and play at cards.

I felt certain that I needed to speak with him, but I could not do so if my aunt could observe it. I did not wish to make her think of the gentleman any more than she already had.

"Do you know anything more about Mr. Bingley's companions?" I asked.

Charlotte's eyebrow rose. "The gentlemen?"

I nodded and took a sip of my punch.

She took a deep breath. "Well, the gentleman at the car table is Mr. Hurst. He is married to one of Mr. Bingley's sisters, though I cannot determine which one..."

I nodded to encourage her, but I did not care about the red-faced gentleman at the card tables.

"And the other— Papa told me that he was very abrupt when he visited Netherfield Park. His name is... Mr. Darcy, I believe. He is not from London, although he may have been at some stage. But he is from much farther north. Derbyshire."

"Indeed," I murmured.

"Mmm. Mama says that he has an income of ten thousand a year, though I would not say that too loudly around these young ladies. Although, I do believe his sour demeanor would frighten anyone away."

"A pity," I said.

"It is," Charlotte agreed. "He is quite handsome, but Mama

thinks him to be an arrogant sort. Even now, he is very aloof. He has not danced at all and I believe I have yet to see him smile."

He was quite handsome, and I felt a little ill as I looked in the gentleman's direction once more. He had, indeed, been the gentleman I'd seen in the park while I walked with my aunt. He had been the inspiration for my dear Mr. Felix Drummond.

Did I dare to speak with him?

"Jane seems to be having a wonderful time with Mr. Bingley," Charlotte observed.

I turned back toward the dance floor and Jane was, indeed, smiling as she went through the steps of the dance with the gentleman in question.

I could detect no bitterness in Charlotte's words and I smiled in return. "It does appear so."

"It would be a good match," Charlotte said. "Mr. Bingley has five thousand a year, according to Mama. Any young lady would be very fortunate to catch his eye. I am not surprised that he has chosen Jane."

"Nor am I," I said.

Charlotte's smile was bright as she slipped her arm through mine. "And what of your own fortunes," she said. "Mama tells me that you are to be married as well!"

My cheeks warmed as I looked away from Charlotte's frank stare in an attempt to appear flustered and demure at the mention of my own engagement. "Indeed, I am," I replied. "Though I do not know when we might be married. He is so often called away on business."

"That is unfortunate," Charlotte said. "Though I imagine that will all come to some sort of conclusion when you are married. Will you settle in London, do you think?"

"Perhaps," I murmured. "We have not discussed it at length."

"There will be time for such things," Charlotte said with a practical air that I had become used to in our discussions. "Until then, you will be able to assist Kitty with preparations for her own marriage. Will she be staying in Meryton?"

"I do not know," I replied. "There has been some talk of Mr. Mason taking on a new role in his father's business, but I have not been included in whatever conversations have taken place about where they will live after their wedding..."

It pained me to admit it, but I had not paid enough attention to anything happening at Longbourn for some time, and I was ashamed of my inattention to Kitty's future. I would have to rectify that as swiftly as possible.

My younger sister was on the dance floor with Mr. Mason, who had finally arrived bearing vehement apologies and a small posy for Kitty that my mother now held.

"It appears, then, that I shall lose all of my friends in Meryton in a short amount of time," Charlotte said with a smile. "I will be quite alone here."

I laughed, though I grew serious after a moment. "I must admit, I will miss you, and our visits."

"Do not worry," Charlotte said. "I will visit you and your new husband in London. You shall grow tired of my visits."

"I do not believe that you will be a spinster," I replied. "Surely, you have some prospects—"

"Oh, I certainly do not," Charlotte exclaimed. "Mama had hoped that there might have been a chance that Mr. Bingley would cast his eye my way, but I do not like the look of him."

I looked over at the dance floor. The gentleman in question was a very... pleasant looking fellow. With a mop of curling fair hair, bright blue eyes, and cheeks that were flushed with the exertion of the dance, or perhaps it was his proximity to Jane. Whatever the cause, it was charming.

"I am sorry to say that he is not to my liking, either," I said. "I prefer darker hair and a darker eye in a man..."

"Like Mr. Darcy," Charlotte observed brightly.

"I—" I glanced back to where Mr. Darcy stood, a stern character amidst the rush of the assembly. "Yes, I suppose so."

"You should go and speak to him," Charlotte said.

"I certainly shall not," I choked out.

"Come now, Lizzy," she said. "He has not danced all evening, which is a capital offense given how many young ladies are without partners tonight. And his friend has danced more than three dances with your own sister... it is the perfect opportunity to do so."

"I do not think so," I said.

The final notes of the dance echoed through the room and I rushed to join the applause of those at the edge of the dance floor as my sister and Mr. Bingley made their way toward us.

The gentleman bowed as Jane introduced him and I found myself liking him immediately. Mr. Bingley was excitable and friendly, and he was easier to talk with than I had expected.

"Have you enjoyed yourself?" I asked Jane as we walked together toward the refreshment table.

Jane nodded. "Indeed, it has been wonderful," she murmured. "Mr. Bingley is very agreeable."

"And you, sir," I asked Mr. Bingley as he ladled punch into glasses for Jane and myself. "Do you find the assembly to your liking? I know it must be nothing to what you are used to in London."

"I find it wonderful," he replied. "I could not ask for a better way to spend an evening than in a dance."

"Why does your friend not join in the merriment," I asked.

Mr. Bingley's smile was more of a grimace as he glanced at his dour friend. "I am afraid that Mr. Darcy does not enjoy such frivolities, I have tried in vain several times to encourage him to take advantage of the evening's entertainments, but he will not."

"It is always a shame when people deny themselves such enjoyment," I observed. "Especially when it is very obvious that there are far too many ladies present tonight... It seems selfish, does it not, Jane?"

"Lizzy—" Jane admonished. "I am certain that Mr. Darcy has a very good reason for avoiding the dancing."

"Certainly not," Mr. Bingley laughed. "I believe Miss Elizabeth has hit upon the very crux of the problem." He turned around and I was shocked to find that Mr. Darcy was standing very close to us, indeed. Close enough that he must have heard what I had said.

I swallowed thickly as his dark gaze passed over me. He seemed angry, but I had insulted him, and I deserved his ire. Though, he should not have been listening to our conversation, and I felt no need to apologize.

"What do you have to say for yourself, Darcy?" Mr. Bingley asked his friend. "What reason could you have for keeping from the dance floor?"

The gentleman's gaze hardened. "You know very well that I do not enjoy social events," he said.

"But, surely," Mr. Bingley said, "for the sake of our arrival here in Hertfordshire you could find some interest in a dance or two?"

"There is no one here who might tempt me," he said. "You have found the prettiest partner to be had. I could not think to compete."

Jane glanced at me—*had he really just been so rude?*

"Come now, Darcy," Mr. Bingley choked out, but his friend had already bowed and taken his leave of us. Mr. Bingley stammered an apology for his friend's rudeness, to which I could only smile. What was I supposed to say?

I had never thought of myself as a vain creature, but his words had cut me deeper than I had expected.

The rest of the evening passed by in a blur, and it was not long before Mr. Bingley, his guests, and his sisters had taken their leave.

My mother and aunt were so pleased by the attention that Mr. Bingley had paid to Jane that she did not seem to recall that there was another gentleman of consequence in attendance that evening.

I wished that I could forget him as well, but his arrogant words were burned into my mind.

What did he mean that there was no one present who might tempt him? Jane had spent a good amount of time on the carriage ride home trying to convince me that he had not intentionally insulted me.

I did not like to hear Jane's defense of the man—Mr. Darcy's words had been terribly rude.

A small part of me wondered if I had deserved such treatment for calling him selfish...

"Come, my dear," my mother said as she shooed us toward our rooms. "It has been a long night, and my feet are aching. We shall speak about the assembly tomorrow. I do believe that I have finally been able to secure a date for Kitty's wedding! Mrs. Mason was very agreeable tonight and I should think that we shall not have long to wait, now."

"But that is wonderful news, Mama," Jane said.

"It is, indeed," our mother exclaimed. "We shall speak more of it in the morning."

I looped my arm through Jane's and we walked up the stairs together. Lydia and Kitty followed us, arguing about something or other as they usually did. Mary had gone up to bed long ago, Papa had been kind enough to allow her to stay home from the assembly, which was a mercy considering how much she disliked such frivolities.

We bid the other girls goodnight and I sighed as we stepped into the bedchamber we had shared since we were very young.

"Will you apologize to Mr. Darcy," Jane asked as she closed the door.

I looked at her in surprise. "I shall not!"

"But, Lizzy..."

"When next I speak to Mr. Darcy it shall be to tell him that he is the rudest man I have ever met and that I have nothing further to say to him."

Jane pressed her fingers to her lips and shook her head. "I believe that he was only flustered by our presence. Mr. Bingley did put him in an awkward position with his question. And you did insult him first."

I let out a huff as I pulled the pins from my hair and set them down upon the vanity. "He said quite plainly that he would not dance because there was no one pretty enough for him to dance with. Except for you, of course."

"Perhaps he is shy," Jane continued. "He does not appear to be very adept at making conversation."

"A gentleman who is too shy for the dance floor?" I exclaimed.

"Perhaps he does not enjoy dancing at all," Jane said.

"Nonsense!" I cried. "He is as arrogant as he is handsome. He has a dreary countenance and I can only imagine that he has an even drearier sense of humor."

Jane laughed at that, but I could sense that she was still upset with me.

"Shall I tell you what I found most appealing about him?" I asked.

"Do not tell me if it is his wealth or his position," Jane said.

"He is so very *tall*."

Jane giggled again.

"In fact, I believe that I have never met anyone so tall, excepting Mr. Kerry, and the parson, of course."

"Did you not describe Mr. Drummond as being tall?" Jane asked with a hint of judgment.

"I did, indeed," I said. "But not so tall as to make me look miniscule at his side! Mr. Darcy is—is..."

"A perfectly acceptable height, and you know it well," Jane said. "Really, Lizzy, you are being quite ridiculous. Mr. Darcy is, by your own admission, handsome enough to tempt even you to reconsider some of your notions about him."

I pulled one last pin from my hair and raked my fingers through my curls. "I suppose so," I said with a sigh. "But even if I did find him agreeable, there is no match to be made there. He said himself that I was not pretty enough for him."

"He did not—"

"You are correct," I replied. "He did not say *precisely* that. I cannot imagine any gentleman saying something so rude and uncalled-for."

"So you will not apologize to Mr. Darcy?" Jane asked.

"No, I shall not," I said as I wrapped my arms around Jane and hugged her tight.

"Perhaps he is not quite so handsome after all," Jane laughed.

"Alongside Mr. Bingley, you mean?" I teased her.

I released my sister from my grasp and sat down upon the edge of my bed as Jane pressed the back of her hand against her flushed cheek. "Mr. Bingley is, indeed, very handsome," she said.

"You would have cherubs for children," I said with a smile. "With curling golden hair and bright blue eyes."

My sister's cheeks flushed just a little more as she stood in front of the vanity to remove the pins and silk flowers from her hair.

"I have been invited to tea at Netherfield Park," Jane said suddenly.

"You have! But Jane, that is wonderful! You did say yes—but of course you did."

"I did," she said. "But you must come with me. Please say that you will."

"Of course," I replied. "I shall not leave you alone with Mr. Bingley's sisters. Goodness knows they looked terrifying..."

"Oh, no," Jane protested. "They were nothing but sweet and welcoming to me when I spoke to them this evening."

"As well they should be," I said. "I cannot imagine that Mr.

Bingley could be in possession of terrible sisters as *well* as a terrible friend. I should begin to doubt my assessment of him!"

Jane made a face at me, but then laughed just a little. "I shall tell Mama in the morning," she said. "She will not argue with this visit."

"I should say not," I exclaimed. "She would never stand in the way of another engagement!"

"Lizzy— You cannot say such things."

"And why not," I demanded. "If I am correct, which is very often, then I predict that Mr. Bingley will come to visit Papa before winter arrives in Hertfordshire."

"You are terrible," Jane sighed.

"In the most wonderful way," I said with a smile as I rose from my seat on the bed and pulled my sleeping robe from the back of the chair where I had hung it before we had departed for the assembly.

"In the morning, Mama will practically insist that you insert yourself into the daily schedule at Netherfield Park so that the servants can be familiar with your likes and dislikes before you become mistress of that estate."

Jane laughed and shook her head. "Terrible."

I was only teasing her, of course, but I could not hide the fact that I had begun to hope that such a thing might be possible, and that I could be free of my false engagement sooner than expected.

Seven

I did not know what to expect from tea with Caroline Bingley and Louisa Hurst... it had been quite some time since I had attended a tea with anyone but my mother and her friends, and their chatter usually washed around me in a way that left me drained and exhausted, but content that I had been utterly forgotten.

This was markedly different.

Caroline Bingley's observations were as sharp as her chin, and she had an opinion about almost everyone of note in Hertford-shire. Including Lady Lucas.

"Now, Jane," Louisa said as another pot of tea was delivered by a wide-eyed maid who rushed from the room as soon as she was dismissed. "I have heard that your sister Kitty is engaged to be married?"

"She is, indeed," Jane replied with a smile.

"Quite sad, do you not think, that a younger sister should be engaged before the elder," Caroline observed. "One would think that should not be the case... but I suppose that with a family so large, and so... overburdened with daughters that it would be a welcome surprise no matter who it might be."

Jane's smile faltered only a little as she stirred her tea.

"We are all very excited for Kitty," she said. "Mr. Mason is a very kind young man, and I know that she will be very happy. They have only just settled upon a date for the happy event."

"How wonderful," Caroline said in a voice that betrayed no cheer whatsoever. "I do not know Mr. Mason myself, but I suppose he must be at least a gentleman of some station: from what I have heard, your father's estate is quite small."

Jane blushed and said nothing in response.

"It is small," I said. "But it provides for us all very well."

"Of course," Caroline murmured. "And Miss Eliza—"

I cringed at the use of that hated nickname.

"Did I not hear that you, yourself are engaged to be married?"

"That is true," Jane said brightly. "Elizabeth is engaged to a lawyer from London."

"How charming," Louisa said. "And what is his name?"

"Mr. Felix Drummond," Jane said before I could stop her. I had not planned to have news of this false engagement spread around any farther than it already had been, but Caroline had already heard some of the gossip...

"Indeed," Louisa said with some interest. "And this Mr. Drummond... What does he look like?"

"Oh," Jane said. "He is quite tall, with dark hair and dark eyes. Very handsome, and with a quick wit to match even Lizzy..."

"Jane," I murmured. My cheeks were hot, and I hoped that the flush in them could be mistaken for something like embarrassment and not abject terror.

"Do we know a Mr. Drummond," Louisa asked thoughtfully. Caroline nodded.

"We do, indeed, but not personally. Though Mr. Darcy would know him quite well..."

"Mr. Darcy?" I asked weakly.

"Why yes, of course," Caroline said. Her voice was sweet and light. "Why, I daresay he mentioned Mr. Felix Drummond not very long ago. I believe he holds an office on South Street—is that not correct Eliza?"

"Forgive me," I said. "But I do not know where his office is. He is so often out of London—."

"Oh, indeed," Caroline said.

I could feel Jane's eyes upon me, but I could not look at her.

"We should ask Mr. Darcy about him," Louisa said. "Surely, Miss Bennet would like to know more about her betrothed!"

"That is not necessary," I stammered.

"Mr. Drummond writes to Lizzy all the time," Jane interjected. "Wonderful letters— there is nothing she does not know about the gentleman."

"Except the location of his offices," Caroline said dryly. She leaned forward in her seat, as though something in the corridor had caught her eye and she rose in a graceful motion and walked quickly toward the door. "Mr. Darcy," she exclaimed. "Could you come into the parlor?"

"I beg your pardon?"

My stomach tightened as the gentleman entered the room. His eyes narrowed as his gaze swept over me.

"We were just speaking of Miss Eliza Bennet's engagement," she said. "To someone that I believe you know quite well."

"Indeed," Mr. Darcy said, his brow furrowing. "To whom?"

"Mr. Felix Drummond," Louisa exclaimed, watching him for any sign of recognition. He simply nodded.

"I would not have thought he had the money to marry," Mr. Darcy said. "He has kept the company of some dubious men."

"Mr. Darcy!" Caroline exclaimed. "Dear Eliza is so happy... I should not like to hear you speak ill of her betrothed!"

He inclined his head. "My apologies, Miss Bennet. I did not mean to cause you any distress with my careless observation."

"Of course not," I murmured.

"But you must tell us more about Mr. Drummond," Caroline pressed. "You must know all there is to know about him,"

"I do," Mr. Darcy said.

Caroline's eyes gleamed. "And so? Is he to inherit a title? A fortune? He cannot just be a lawyer—"

"He is just a lawyer," Mr. Darcy confirmed. "A goodly one at that. Although I am surprised that you might have met him, Miss Bennet. He is not often in London—"

"It was quite an accident," I said in a rush.

"Indeed, their courtship was swift as well," Jane said. "It was not more than a fortnight after their meeting that Mr. Drummond made his offer of marriage!"

I gritted my teeth and wished that I could nudge my sister into silence, but I could not.

"I see," he said and he stared at me for a long moment before he turned his gaze back to Caroline. "If you will excuse me, I was on my way to the stables."

"Of course," Caroline sighed. "You have told me nothing interesting whatsoever." She waved her hand in dismissal and the gentleman bowed and strode toward the parlor door.

When he disappeared into the corridor, I was struck with a sudden thought—I needed to speak with Mr. Darcy immediately.

"Lizzy—"

"I believe I would like to take some air," I blurted out. I set my teacup down as I stood. "I shall return in a moment, I just need to... clear my head."

"Lizzy, are you quite well?" Jane's expression was full of concern.

"Yes— it is just far too warm in here," I said. "I shall be back in a moment. You will not even miss me."

I rushed from the room before I could be commanded to stay. Mr. Darcy was going to the stables, and I would have to follow him.

I stopped one of the servants to ask them where the stables were, and followed their surprised directions as well as I was able and finally found the door that would take me to the path that led down toward the stables.

I could hear the gentleman's footsteps ahead of me and I quickened my pace until I could see the pale gray of his jacket through the trees.

"Mr. Darcy," I called out.

The gentleman paused and turned toward me.

"Miss Bennet—"

Out of breath, and feeling flustered, I stopped just short of him and pressed my hands against my skirts.

He waited for me to speak, but I did not know what to say.

"I—"

"You are engaged to Mr. Drummond," he said. "I find that very hard to believe."

I straightened my shoulders. "And why is that?"

"Mr. Felix Drummond is almost sixty years old."

I froze in place.

"I—"

"So, you would tell me that Mr. Felix Drummond, a lawyer from London who has been twice widowed, and keeps offices on South Road met you, fell madly in love with you, and asked you to marry him within a fortnight of your meeting."

My mouth opened and closed but no sound came out.

The gentleman's mouth twisted in something that resembled a smile. "I see."

"This is not what it seems," I protested. "If you will just let me explain—."

"There is no need," he said. "I understand very well."

"But it is not what you think," I said. "It is... the engagement is not *real*."

"Which only makes your situation worse." He shook his head. "What amazes me is that you are not ashamed."

I frowned at him. "If you will allow me a moment to gather my thoughts I believe that I can make everything clear to you."

"There is nothing to be made clear," he said. "Your engagement is to a gentleman old enough to be your father, for what purpose? Money? Are your family's circumstances so dire that you would accept any offer of marriage no matter who has made it?"

Anger prickled up my spine.

"You do not know me, or my family," I snapped. "The engagement is not real because I have never met Mr. Felix Drummond."

He blinked at me.

"I beg your pardon?"

I had no intention of telling Mr. Darcy that it was *he* who had inspired my descriptions of the false gentleman. But the rest? What harm could it do to tell him? I would need for him to understand if I was to gain his assistance.

"Mr. Felix Drummond, the gentleman my sister spoke of, is a fabrication. The Mr. Drummond I am engaged to is a fantasy that I concocted to keep my mother from arranging a marriage to the first gentleman who might express an interest in me." Thankfully, the gentleman's surprise at my admission had struck him silent. "So," I continued, "you are not entirely incorrect in your insults, Mr. Darcy, but I do not deserve such scorn."

"I—"

Now it was his turn to be speechless.

"I merely wish to be left alone," I said. "And this was the only way I could think of to bring such a thing about. I have four sisters, Mr. Darcy. My mother is obsessed with our futures, and rightly so. We are not a wealthy family, but I could not bear the pressure of it any longer—"

"So you have... invented a fiancé to distract your mother?"

I bit my lip and nodded. "It seemed the easiest way to do so. She was distracted by my younger sister's engagement and plans for her wedding. It was that, or be forced to marry the first man she pointed out to me in a ballroom."

"And you have confided in your sister."

I glanced away. "Yes. And my father."

He closed his eyes and shook his head, his expression one of mild disgust.

"And how long did you plan to keep this... fiction intact?"

I twisted my fingers together. "I have not— That is to say—"

"And what reason, Miss Bennet, do you have for telling me all of this," he interrupted me.

"I had hoped that you would... help me."

He laughed, short and sharp. "Help you?"

I nodded. "Miss Bingley said that you know Mr. Drummond — Would you be able to, if necessary, pretend to know *my* Mr. Drummond?"

"*Your* Mr. Drummond."

"The one that I have fabricated," I continued. "Could you pretend to know him and lend legitimacy to my story? It need only be once... a simple confirmation—"

"I am not an actor, Miss Bennet," he snapped.

"Nor would you have to be," I said. "I will provide all of the information you require... all you need do is confirm that you know him."

His mouth twisted.

"No."

Before I could stop myself, I reached out and grabbed hold of his elbow. I released it only half a moment later, but the look of surprise on his face sent a shiver through me.

"Please, will you consider it?"

I did not want to beg, but it was impossible not to.

"And if I refuse?"

"Then you have lost nothing," I said. "When my mother discovers the falsehood, there is nothing to protect me from the gossip or the scandal that would come from such a confession."

He seemed to consider my words carefully. "And if I agree? What would be required of me?"

I could not help the smile that spread across my face. "I will bring you the letters that I have written so that you might familiarize yourself with the gentleman I have invented. I would only ask that you come to supper at Longbourn—as Mr. Drummond's friend—and lend legitimacy to my claims."

"I see."

"Nothing else," I said. "And I shall bother you no more."

His eyebrow rose. "Is that a promise?"

"It is," I replied.

Mr. Darcy favored me with a brief smile that made my heart lurch in my chest.

Hope.

"I will consider it," he said.

"Oh!"

He turned away. "Good day, Miss Bennet."

"Mr. Darcy— When... when will you decide?"

He didn't answer and I stood on the path, frustrated, my hands balled into fists at my sides as I watched him walk down the path and disappear between the trees.

"Infuriating," I muttered.

A brisk wind blew through the trees and I wrapped my arms around myself against the sudden chill and I turned and ran back toward the house.

Eight

I spent a furious few days wondering if I had made the biggest mistake of my life by bringing a gentleman I hardly knew into my confidence. I had a wild hope that perhaps he would just disregard our interaction and I could continue with my life without his acknowledgement. Besides—when would my mother ever hear that Mr. Darcy was acquainted with Mr. Drummond?

But as much as I tried to reassure myself, it was never enough. Caroline Bingley was the object of every one of Lady Lucas' conversations, and I knew that she longed to be invited to tea as Jane was. The prospect of the most notorious gossip in Hertfordshire taking tea with Miss Bingley was something that filled me with a certain amount of fear.

A very certain amount.

Jane continued to visit Netherfield Park, and my mother's anticipation of a third marriage proposal seemed as though it grew with each passing hour.

But on one particular day, when I was trying to decide between forgetting about Mr. Darcy altogether and returning to plead my case to the aloof gentleman, Jane returned from Netherfield Park with a strange flush to her cheeks.

"Lizzy," she hissed, "I must speak with you."

I followed her down the corridor and she looked nervously over my shoulder to be certain that no one had followed us as she pulled something from her reticule.

"Jane.. what is this?"

My sister's gaze burned into mine. "A note from Mr. Darcy," she whispered. "What is going on, Lizzy?"

I plucked the note from her fingers and broke the seal with nervous fingers.

Why would the gentleman risk some small scandal by sending me a message?

Miss Bennet, I believe we have more to speak of. If you will bring your correspondence to Netherfield Park, I shall look it over.

-D

My breath caught and I looked up at my sister.

"What is it?"

"I—"

"Lizzy—" Her tone held some warning and I forced myself to smile.

"It is nothing," I said and then remembered that Jane would have to know of this as well. "No... That is not true. I begged Mr. Darcy to intervene on my behalf—"

Jane's eyes widened. "In what?"

"In this fiction about Mr. Drummond," I hissed.

"Lizzy, this has taken a new turn," Jane exclaimed. I hushed her as best I could.

"It is necessary," I said. "I do not trust Caroline Bingley—"

Jane let out a derisive snort. "But you do not even know her!"

"Neither do you," I replied. "Has she said anything about how she might speak to her brother about you?"

"Well..."

"If the answer is no, just say so," I said.

Jane let out a short breath. Frustration.

"She has spoken often about Mr. Darcy's sister and how fond they are of her."

"And I do suppose that Miss Bingley wishes that her brother would make a proposal of marriage to Miss Darcy?"

I did not intend the bitterness that I heard in my own voice, and I saw its recognition in Jane's expression. I wanted to apologize, but she recovered quickly.

"Miss Darcy is no older than Kitty," she said. "Surely, you cannot believe that he might—"

"No, indeed," I said. "He would be a bald-faced fool to consider that match." I laid a comforting hand upon my sister's cheek. "You are perfect, Jane. Perfect for him. And I know that he sees it, too."

Jane smiled and took hold of my hand and pulled it away from her face. "What did Mr. Darcy say—"

"He has agreed to help me," I said, but then I re-read his note. "Although, he doesn't not expressly say such a thing."

"Then what are you to do?"

"I suppose I shall bring all of the letters I have written from Mr. Drummond," I said. "When are you to go to Netherfield Park next?"

Jane frowned, but only for a moment. "Tomorrow," she replied. "Would you have me deliver the letters? If so, I must decide how I will explain my wish to see Mr. Darcy—"

"No, no," I said. "I shall come with you. I shall go to Mr. Darcy immediately, and then return to Longbourn. Caroline and Louisa need never know that I was there."

"You are certain?" Her tone held a note of both approval and concern. "There is no need to stir more trouble, Lizzy. What do you think they might do if they learned of this?"

My cheeks burned at that. If they discovered the truth, my reputation in Hertfordshire would be ruined. Even though my actions and choices did not affect her in the slightest, Miss Bingley seemed like the sort of woman who would not rest until I was well and truly shamed for my lies.

"I shall have to be sure that they do not discover it," I said with a hasty smile. "I shall accompany you to Netherfield Park tomorrow, and I shall tell you everything when you return home."

Jane sighed heavily. "If you insist."

"Do not worry for me, dearest," I said. "You only need think about one thing, and that is securing a favorable mention from Miss Bingley or Mrs. Hurst to their brother. Although I do not think that Mr. Bingley will need any convincing of his affection for you. You do walk in the gardens after tea, do you not?"

Jane's cheeks flushed as she smiled. "We do, almost every time I visit."

"And have you spoken of marriage?"

Jane shook her head. "Almost everything *but*," she exclaimed. "I know how many children he wishes to have—boys and girls— and where he would wish to spend the summers and Christmastide—" Jane smiled. "And I have even been able to mention that I wish to have you stay as governess to my children."

My heart skipped a beat. "and what did he say?"

"He thought it a wonderful idea," she said with a smile. "Who would be better to teach the children?"

"I am so pleased that he is in agreement!" But nothing was certain... not yet. The fact that Mr. Bingley was speaking of marriage in an indirect way was something of a triumph, but he had not yet spoken of it *directly*... which meant that he was held to nothing.

Yet.

"You shall have to give some thought to a wedding gown," I whispered. "I feel that Mr. Bingley will soon ask for your hand in marriage."

I gave Jane a quick kiss upon her cheek.

"You must go back to the parlor," I said. "Our mother will want to have a detailed account of your teatime visit with Mr. Bingley's sisters."

"As ever," Jane sighed.

"I must go and sort my letters," I said. I gripped her hands in mine and squeezed gently. "Tomorrow I shall secure Mr. Darcy's support, and with any luck we may abandon this charade in short order."

"Perhaps," Jane said with a shy smile. I hoped that she did not feel any pressure to choose Mr. Bingley, but it seemed that she held him in very high esteem already.

Jane pulled away from me and entered the parlor just as my mother began to call for her. They would be preoccupied until supper, which gave me time to sort through the letters for the ones that would be most helpful to provide Mr. Darcy with a clear portrait of the Mr. Drummond that I had created in my mind.

I clutched his note tightly in my hand as I rushed up to the bedchamber I shared with Jane. Tomorrow this would all be set right. Tomorrow I would have confirmation that my ruse was believable.

$\sim$

A knot of anticipation curled in my stomach as I knocked upon Mr. Darcy's door.

Jane was already seated in the parlor with Miss Bingley and Mrs. Hurst, and I had avoided detection by Mr. Bingley's sisters by only a small margin.

I had been informed by a very helpful footman that Mr. Darcy was in Netherfield Park's drawing room.

I did not wait for him to answer my knock, and after only a moment's pause I twisted the knob and opened the door. The gentleman stood behind a large mahogany desk that was strewn with books and papers. He was dressed in a plain riding coat and a shirt that had been hastily tucked in. His curling dark hair was wild, as though he had raked his hand through it only recently, and his eyes blazed as I entered the room.

"What on earth—"

"I apologize for interrupting you," I whispered. "But your note — I could not delay."

I could hear the chatter of Miss Bingley's laughter in the parlor, as well as the clack of mah-jong tiles as Mrs. Hurst and Jane played a game of it. I closed the door behind me, shutting out the sound of their voices.

He looked me up and down, his eyes roving over my form as though he could not believe what he was seeing.

"I would prefer to speak to you later," he hissed.

I shook my head emphatically. "No. Now," I said.

He waved me into the room and I pulled the stack of letters from my cloak.

His eyes widened as I set them down upon his desk.

"There," I said firmly. "There is everything that you need to know about Mr. Drummond."

"You... you wrote all of these?"

I nodded. "All of them. This was how I was to prove that the engagement was real."

He untied the dark blue silk ribbon that I had tied around the bundle and selected the first one.

He opened it and scanned it carefully, his eyes racing hungrily across the page. He paused for just a moment, glanced at me, and grabbed hold of the rest of the pile. He walked to the couch that had been pulled in front of the fire and sat down.

He placed the stack of letters down on the cushion beside him and flipped through the letters with the swiftness of one used to reading.

I sank down into a nearby chair and watched him as he read. Every so often, he would glance over at me, and I noticed more than once that his mouth twisted into something that could be mistaken for a smile.

"And you imagined... all of this?"

"I did," I replied.

"This is— Mr. Drummond's history is not based upon anyone that you might know?"

"No, indeed," I laughed. "If it were, I should much prefer to be engaged to *him*. I know that he does not exist, and so I have gifted my dear false Fiancé with all of the qualities I might hope for in a husband."

"Including being away from you for long periods of time?"

I shifted in my seat. "Well, that has only been ideal for this particular situation," I said. "If I were to marry, that would not be what I wished for. Of course. But such a thing is not up for discussion."

He looked back at the letters and continued reading.

The silence between us was heavy, and I found myself fearing that I had said too much. I did not know this gentleman... And the fact that I was seated in the drawing room alone with him was entirely scandalous. Were anyone to discover us, it would be ruinous—

But I could not think of such a thing. He had offered to help me, I could not believe that he would betray the trust I had put in him.

"These letters are ridiculous, you know," he said suddenly.

I sat up a little straighter at his tone. "I beg your pardon?"

"These letters," he held one up, "a gentleman would never write something like this."

I crossed my arms over my chest and glared at him. "Oh, indeed?"

"Indeed," he retorted. "No gentleman would ever speak about the color of your eyes, or how he believes they might sparkle in the sun when next you meet—"

I said nothing.

"He might compliment your eyes, and say that they are fine—But this? This is far too descriptive! It is almost—"

"Mr. Drummond has a way with words that you could not comprehend, and a love of poetry," I snapped, interrupting him. "Do you have an issue with it?"

He snorted and shook his head. "None at all. What poets does he favor so that I might not insult them—"

"He favors the classic Greek poets," I said at once. "And he can read their words in the original language without hesitation or need for assistance with pronunciation."

"And Latin as well?"

"Of course."

His eyebrow rose and he opened another letter and continued to read.

I could not help but smile as I watched him.

He tilted his head this way and that, and he kept the stack of letters beside him in a neat pile. One read, re-folded carefully, the other still primly folded waiting for his scrutiny.

As he read, his eyes kept returning to me. I did not know what he was reading— But whatever it was, he seemed to find it amusing.

"Is there something you find intriguing in the letters," I asked abruptly.

He paused and tapped the edge of the letter he held upon his palm. "Intriguing? Several things, actually," he replied. "Tell me, Miss Elizabeth," he said quietly. "Are you very certain that you did not base this version of Mr. Felix Drummond upon anyone else of your acquaintance?"

I shook my head. "I have already confirmed that is not the case," I said. "Everything you are reading is entirely a work of fiction. From his family to his affinity for the Classic poets. A fabrication."

"And your reason for fabricating such a character—"

"I have also already explained," I said. My cheeks were warm. "Mr. Darcy, if you do not wish to assist me, then I shall ask that you return the letters and forget that you we have ever spoken of such a thing—"

I rose from my chair, but he held up a hand to stop me. "I do apologize," he said. "Please, I should like to finish reading."

I sank slowly down into the chair once more and folded my hands in my lap.

He nodded and returned to reading.

I watched him carefully, and I waited for his opinion with bated breath. He was, after all, the last hope that I had to find some sort of a way to legitimize this false engagement, which had become something very unlike what I had intended.

After what seemed like hours, he placed the last letter upon the stack and looked up at me.

"And so," I said. "Do you have an accurate impression of Mr. Drummond?"

"I do."

"And you have no further questions?"

He pulled the stack of letters into his lap and tied the silk ribbon around them once more. "You have mentioned nothing about his supposed personal habits?"

"He is a gentleman," I said. "He conducts himself in a manner commensurate with his station. He does not gamble, he does not drink overmuch... I suspect that he might enjoy shooting, although I would hope that he would have a tender heart and would not enjoy the act of killing... but the fresh air and the company of other gentlemen is a welcome respite from his work."

"You have given this gentleman a great deal of thought."

"As does every young girl when she imagines what her husband might be like," I replied.

His smile was brief.

"I see. And... Do all young women do this?"

I shrugged. "All the ones I know."

"And how often is it that these young women are able to marry the gentleman they have dreamed of?"

I snorted. "It would be kinder to ask how many of them are happy in their marriages."

"I see."

He held the stack of letters out to me and I rose from my chair to retrieve them.

"I hope that I did not offend you, Miss Bennet, it was not my intention. Nor to make light of—" He frowned.

"You did not," I said. And it was true, while he had been rude, I was not offended or angry with him. What confused me, however, was how willing I was to be honest with him. I should not have been—

"I shall assist you," he said, "if you will have it."

"I will," I said. "And I thank you. I admit, I am almost surprised."

"Surprised?"

I nodded and tucked the letters back into my cloak. "I had expected that you might laugh at me—and at my efforts. I did not expect that you would be willing to assist me."

He rose from the couch and I straightened my shoulders as he towered over me. *He was entirely too tall for my liking... Or... was he?*

"And why do you suppose I might have refused?" he asked.

I forced myself to smile as I walked past him toward the drawing room door. "There is no need for you to assist," I said. "You do not know me, I am not one of your relations in need of charity or saving— and I am certainly no one of consequence."

"On the contrary," he said. "If you have won the heart of my dear friend, Felix, then I would say that you are quite remarkable, indeed."

My cheeks burned and I shook my head. "I shall send word," I said. "Will you come to dinner at Longbourn? And bring Mr. Bingley?"

His eyebrow rose slightly. "Mr. Bingley?"

I nodded. "My sister, Jane, is quite—" I paused, wondering if I should press for something that I knew Jane would wish for but would never ask for herself. "She would very much like to see Mr. Bingley away from his sisters."

"I believe I take your meaning," Mr. Darcy replied. "Send word, and I shall do my best to encourage his attendance."

"Without mentioning the request came from me..."

He inclined his head. "Of course."

"Thank you," I said and then pressed my ear to the drawing room door.

"What are you doing?"

"Listening to see if there is anyone in the corridor," I said shortly. "I cannot be seen. I was not supposed to be here today. Miss Bingley and Mrs. Hurst do not know that I am here."

"And you do not wish to see them?"

"No, I do not," I hissed.

The gentleman's chuckle caught me off guard, and I pulled the door open. "I shall send word through Jane," I said. "Good day, Mr. Darcy."

I did not wait for his reply and slipped out of the room and into the corridor.

I had to rush through the halls without running, lest I fall—and run into someone I did not want to see.

My skirts were hiked high to avoid sweeping against the wall and I nearly tripped once or twice.

Thankfully, the corridors were empty, and I escaped to the outside of the house without being seen.

I hiked my skirts a bit more and ran down the drive toward the main road.

My face was still warm, but I did not care.

I was satisfied that my scheme would work. And now I had the support of Mr. Darcy to lend weight to my fiction.

I could only hope that his words would keep my mother distracted until Jane received an offer of marriage from Mr. Bingley.

Perhaps bringing him to Longbourn for supper would hasten things along.

Nine

"**Y**ou did *what*?"

Jane's voice was not quiet, and I was thankful that we were alone in the gardens to gather some herbs for Mrs. Hill's beef stew.

"Jane—" I hissed. "Keep your voice down."

"I most certainly will *not*," she snapped. "Explain yourself at once!"

"I spoke to Mr. Darcy," I said. "As you very well know. I gave him the letters to look over to familiarize himself with the character of the gentleman I have created—"

"And you invited him to supper here at Longbourn.."

"Yes, I—"

"*And* Mr. Bingley!"

"Jane— you must not be cross with me—"

"Cross," Jane choked out. "I do not even know how I should feel! Lizzy, why have you done this? It's highly improper for a young lady to make such a request!"

"Everything I have done in the last few *months* has been improper," I said. "But I cannot take any of it back."

"But why must you involve—"

"Do you wish for Mr. Bingley to make a proposal of marriage?" I asked.

Jane stopped, her cheeks pink and her blue eyes wide. "I— Of course I do."

"And you would accept it if he did propose?"

"Of course, Lizzy, but I do not—"

"Mr. Darcy has agreed to help me," I said. "The only way that he will be able to do such a thing is if he is able to come to supper."

Jane glared at me. "And how will you secure his invitation?"

"Papa has already agreed to send one," I said. "It is all arranged."

"I see."

"Jane, you would not fault me if you could have seen Mr. Darcy as he read my letters," I said. "He mocked me for their contents at first."

"Which parts?"

"The poets," I said with a smile. "He did not believe that a gentleman would write such things in his letters to a young lady."

"I see— And what did you make of Mr. Darcy himself during this... meeting?"

I could not be certain if Jane's humor had improved, but I forged ahead.

"He is dry, and very dull," I said. "And so very disagreeable that he insulted me within the first few minutes of our conversation. It is no great surprise to me that he is as yet unmarried."

"Indeed," she said.

I took my sister's hand and squeezed it gently. "Please do not be cross with me," I said. "I was only thinking of you."

Jane's smile was brief and I was not convinced that she was not upset with me. My father had promised to send the invitation, and my mother would be alerted in good time. Time enough, of course, for her to tell all of her friends about the important visitors who would be coming to Longbourn.

The dinner would be held in a fortnight—and I would have to put aside my anxiety until then.

～

The anticipation of the dinner put me on edge, but Jane was still receiving invitations to Netherfield Park, and even though I still suspected that she was angry with me, she still wanted me to come with her.

I couldn't abandon Jane to the tiger's den that Netherfield Park's parlor had become under Caroline and Louisa's imperious stares.

The supper was only a few days away, and I had spoken with Mr. Darcy on several occasions since our first meeting. He had asked me questions about Mr. Drummond, and I had found myself, against my will, enjoying his company.

But as the date of the supper drew nearer, my mother had been informed of the guests who would be joining us for supper, which meant that the entirety of Hertfordshire also knew.

Including Caroline Bingley.

The visit began as it usually did, but Jane walked ahead of me down the corridor.

As Jane entered the parlor, I realized that I was not alone in the corridor. Caroline Bingley, her sharp eyes glittering in the dim light, approached me.

"Miss Eliza Bennet—"

"Caroline," I said with a smile. "I do hope that you are well this afternoon."

"I am very well, indeed," she said. Her smile was catlike and nothing about it was friendly. "I have heard that you will be receiving guests at Longbourn."

"We are, indeed," I said.

I could only stay calm and pleasant with Caroline. It would be too easy to slip into harshness and biting comments—but I could not bring myself to descend to the level that she was so comfortable with.

"I will not be coy about this, Eliza," she hissed. "I do not believe for one moment that Mr. Darcy would be a close confidant of the gentleman that you have described with such eager and flowery words."

My throat tightened, but I did my best to keep my smile intact. Caroline would be looking for any waver, any hint that I was not entirely honest. She would see deception even if there was none— but there was a great deal of it here...

"Do you believe so?" I managed to say.

"I shall find the truth of it," Caroline said. "And when I do, I shall expose you, and I shall tell my brother that he cannot consider your sister as his bride. How could I stand by when our family is to be aligned with one so dishonest?"

"There is nothing dishonest about Jane," I said firmly. "And you shall be disappointed in your search for deception."

I had to believe it.

I had to hope that everything would be resolved sooner than later.

"I do hope that you are mistaken," she said with a smile. "I feel that Mr. Darcy would have alerted us to the fact that a gentleman existed who was so like himself— A veritable twin."

"I— I do not take your meaning."

I regarded Caroline with genuine disbelief.

"Do you mean to tell me that your dear Mr. Drummond did not once mention Mr. Darcy in his letters? They are dear friends, are they not? Having grown up in similar circumstances— and with almost identical tastes and interests. Come now, Eliza—"

I forced myself to smile, though my stomach was tight and a cold chill had taken hold of me. "He did not," I said as calmly as I could. "But I feel certain that the subject would have presented itself eventually."

"Eventually," Caroline said with a smooth smile. She glanced at the parlor door. "Come, Eliza," she said. "We must not keep our dear sister's waiting."

"No, indeed," I replied.

We entered the parlor together, and Jane looked at me with an expression of concern in her eyes, but there was nothing I could do but greet Louisa and take my place on the couch beside Jane as the mah-jong tiles were set out.

I was hopeless at this game, but Jane had an affinity for it that I envied.

"I will just watch this round," I said as I poured myself a cup of tea.

I could feel Caroline's eyes upon me, and I wondered if she had spoken any of her poison into her sister's ears.

Undoubtedly.

Perhaps this was all wrong. Perhaps I had overstepped.

What if the very thing I was attempting to secure was undone by my own actions?

Jane would forgive me if Mr. Bingley did not propose... but I would never forgive myself.

~

I was quite certain that I was doomed.

It was nearly supper time, and Jane and I were in the garden to collect flowers for the table, but Jane had barely spoken to me since she had learned of what Caroline had said.

She had been uncharacteristically quiet, and I had resigned myself to the fact that she was still angry with me. And she had good reason to be.

I had jeopardized the very freedom I had hoped to gain.

But, worst of all, I had allowed Caroline's poisonous words to enter my mind.

My mind raced with possibilities, but I knew that there was naught I could do to correct anything that had happened. Caroline had threatened the very worst, but I did not know if she would be able to find the evidence she so desperately sought. She could not go to her brother with empty accusations.

But if she did discover what she was looking for she would use it as an opportunity to destroy me... and Jane.

Caroline would do her very best to see that the truth was spread all through Hertfordshire... I would never be received in society again, and our family would be all but ruined. Mr. Mason would likely end his engagement to Kitty, and Lydia and Jane's prospects would be ruined.

And it would be all my fault.

"Lizzy— you do not look well at all," Jane said suddenly.

"Oh?"

"Are you thinking about Caroline Bingley again?"

I nodded as Jane took my hand and squeezed my fingers. "Do not think of her," she said. "Miss Bingley is... misunderstood, I think. But I cannot deny that she was very cruel to you. She means to protect her brother, and their family from scandal. But there is no scandal to be found."

I tried to smile, but it was difficult.

"You are not angry with me, are you?" I asked.

Jane shook her head. "No. At first, when you told me what you had done I *was* angry. But as the days have gone by, I am encouraged by Mr. Bingley's attendance. Mama has sent Lydia and Mary away to dine with Lady Lucas..."

"It was a wonderful suggestion," I said.

Jane deserved all the credit for how this evening had developed.

My father had been encouraged to invite Mr. Mason to supper as well in the hope that there could be a sort of comfort in having an already engaged couple in the house to distract our mother long enough to avoid any discomfort.

It would not be a complete victory, but it would be enough.

And if I knew our mother, she would find a way to bring some discomfort to the forefront before long.

The gentlemen's arrival was met with my mother's cries of delight—Mr. Mason was first to arrive in his second best carriage, and Mr. Bingley and Mr. Darcy arrived on horseback from Netherfield Park.

Mr. Darcy was as stoic as I had expected, but I was grateful that Mr. Bingley seemed eager to be there and I took some solace in the fact that if he *had* listened to his sister, he had done so with a mind to her cruelty and a desire to make his own opinion.

That was my hope at least.

The dining room had been prepared with an eye to detail that Jane had overseen, even though our mother made a grand display of approving everything that she had already accomplished.

I did worry that Mr. Darcy would be a dull dinner guest, but thankfully the pressure had been lifted from him by the other gentlemen, and my father's unexpectedly lively participation in the events of the evening.

The conversation flowed easily enough, as both Mr. Mason and Mr. Bingley were surprisingly calm and affable. Both men were charming, and Mr. Bingley was particularly attentive to Jane, which made my mother's happy reactions enough to border on ridiculous.

At a lull between dishes, my mother suddenly seemed to remember that there was another gentleman present.

"Mr. Darcy," she exclaimed. "I have been told that you have a good knowledge of Mr. Drummond— You know that he is to be married to my dear Lizzy!"

"I do, indeed," Mr. Darcy replied.

He met my eyes briefly, and I could feel my heart race as he gave me a small smile.

"I have had the good fortune of speaking to Mr. Drummond on many occasions through correspondence and in person," he said. "We have been friends for a great many years, and I am pleased to be acquainted with a man whose character is so amiable and pleasant. He is fortunate indeed to have met your daughter."

My father smiled as he looked down at his place, and my mother's face beamed with pride as Jane glanced in my direction.

"But you must tell us more of him," my mother exclaimed. "I feel as though I know him very well from his letters, but you have known him in person—"

Before she could say more, Mr. Bingley interjected. "I think you must tell us more of Mr. Drummond, Mr. Darcy," he said. "Your familiarity with Mr. Drummond must be a happy one."

"Of course," Mr. Darcy said with a nod.

He sat up straight, and I watched him with interest. "Mr. Drummond is a man of very fine character," he said. "His father was a friend of my own father as it happens. My father knew of our friendship, and before his death he entrusted Mr. Drummond with a great deal of money and the entirety of his business dealings."

"Oh!" My mother's exclamation sounded sharp in the silence of the room, and I tightened my grip on my fork. Mr. Darcy and I had not discussed everything that he might say this evening, but this was certainly not on the list of possible topics—and he was embellishing far too much.

"I must say with a certain degree of pride that my friend has excelled in his handling of them. His integrity, and prudence is admirable, and I could not be more pleased for him and his engagement to your daughter. He is a man of character and judgment, and I know that you will enjoy his company as much as I do. Though, he does have an overfondness for the classic poets—"

The gentleman glanced at me and I pressed my lips together to keep from snapping at him. He did delight in vexing me.

My father broke in. "Mr. Drummond certainly enjoys a fine reputation," he said. "Am I correct, Mr. Darcy, that Mr. Drummond is a man who can command the attention of an entire room with just one word?"

"I do not know that to be true, sir," Mr. Darcy replied. "He is a quiet sort of gentleman who is not given to such displays. His father was a commanding presence, but my friend is a more subdued version of that great man. My own father was especially fond of him, and I have always found him to be pleasant and kind." He paused a moment before he continued.

My mother smiled, her eyes wide with excitement. "What a wonderful match," she said. "It will be a great pleasure to have Mr. Drummond as part of the family."

"Indeed," Mr. Darcy said with a smile. He raised his wine glass and the others at the table followed suit with such speed that I was forced to drop my fork to keep pace. I should have been the first one to take up my glass, but I was the last and my mother fixed me with a stern glare as Mr. Darcy rose.

"A toast," he said. "To the happy union of two young people who are so aligned in their wit, honesty, and temperament. I have no doubt that their match will be a happy one."

"Here, here," Mr. Bingley said loudly, but his gaze lingered upon Jane and I wondered with some breathless hope that he might be considering another match...

"I almost forgot," Mr. Darcy said suddenly as dessert was set upon the table. "Mr. Drummond bid me deliver a gift."

"A gift," my mother exclaimed.

I met the gentleman's gaze with confusion. We had not discussed this at all.

"A gift?"

"Indeed," he said. He brought forth a package wrapped in a dark velvet cloth and Kitty gasped aloud.

"Oh, Lizzy," she hissed. "It is a book—"

I knew the look of a gift like this well enough. I received books for my birthday, Christmas, and any other holiday imaginable... It was the one gift that my family knew would be received with a smile.

But what had Mr. Darcy brought me?

It was difficult not to be suspicious as I took the package that Mr. Darcy passed across the table to me.

I unwrapped the velvet carefully and glanced up at him as I did so. His expression was neutral, as though he had not just given me a very public gift—but everyone at the table, aside from Jane and my father, would believe that it had come from Mr. Drummond.

"Byron!" Kitty declared. "You do love him, Lizzy. His works are so very scandalous and passionate!"

The volume was newly published and I rubbed my hand over the smooth leather of the front cover. The scent of the paper and fresh binding invaded my senses and I fought to keep my composure.

Childe Harold's Pilgrimage

An extravagant gift... and one I did not feel that I deserved.

"I—"

"Lizzy, you must write to Mr. Drummond immediately," my mother said. "Such a wonderful gift, and so unexpected. The gentleman is in Paris, after all. Surely, you might have told him that a parasol or a fan might have been an appropriate gift—"

"Do you like it?" Mr. Darcy asked.

"I— I am overwhelmed," I managed.

"Felix will wish to know of your reaction when you received it, and I should like to tell him that you were overjoyed—although—"

I smiled at him. "I am. Exceedingly. And you may convey that to him." I turned to my mother. "I will, indeed, write to him at once, Mama."

"Good," she said with a self-satisfied smile. There could have been many gifts that would have highlighted my false fiancé's wealth and prestige, but a new printing of a book of poetry was... perfect. No one could doubt that it had been freshly printed and I wondered how many copies had been made.

As my sisters exclaimed over the book, my father's smile had taken on a strange quality—one that made me notice how he regarded Mr. Darcy.

This gift was one that he had chosen for me—very specifically

—and I was not certain of how I felt about this sudden development, but there was no mistaking the way my cheeks warmed as I opened the volume and saw the gentleman's elegant handwriting.

For Elizabeth

Oh... dear.

Ten

Weeks passed and, as I had hoped, Mr. Darcy's presence at supper, and his glowing endorsement of Mr. Drummond had only fuelled my mother's support for the union I had fabricated.

I continued to write letters from the gentleman who did not exist, but for some reason, every time I wrote them, I imagined not what he might say... but what Mr. Darcy might write. He had mocked me for the content of my letters, saying that they were not what a gentleman might compose... But I suspected that was not the case.

The book he had brought me lay upon my night table, and though I had read it at least a dozen times, each time I wondered what he might think of it, and what his own impressions would be of the poet's mindset as he wrote it.

I liked to imagine that the ancient poets delighted themselves, or dinner guests, with their recitations before applying ink to page —but this? This was a work of deeply felt passion that moved me in different ways every time I read it.

Had Mr. Darcy been similarly affected by it? Or had he only gifted it to me because I mentioned that I enjoyed poetry. Or, was he simply mocking me again by attempting to show me what "real" poetry was?

If it was the latter, then I should return the volume and confront his insult.

Yes, that could be the only answer.

"Lizzy! You must come at once, there is a package for you!"

Kitty's shout echoed up the stairs and I rose from my seat at the small desk that had been placed under the window in the bedchamber I shared with Jane.

As I reached the door, I could hear her arguing with Lydia.

"No! You must not open it, it is not for you!"

"Come now," Lydia hissed. "She will not know—"

"She will know if you rip the paper, Lydia!"

The sound of their struggle brought a smile to my face. Whatever change would come into our lives, there were some things that could be depended upon never to change. The rivalry between my younger sisters was one of those things.

As I descended the stairs, I watched them tug a paper-wrapped object between them.

"Whatever are you doing?" I asked.

Kitty's cheeks were pink as she wrenched the package from Lydia's hands. The paper tore and she wailed in despair as Lydia laughed.

"Lizzy, look," she cried. "A parasol!"

Kitty's eyes were filled with tears as she handed the partially unwrapped parcel to me. "I am sorry—"

"Do not worry," I said with a smile. "You know how much I dislike surprises."

Kitty's answering smile was a little crooked, and then she glared at Lydia. "It is from Mr. Drummond," she said. "The parasol that you wanted from Paris!"

The only mention of the parasol had been at supper, and I gritted my teeth at the memory of how my mother had mentioned it.

How grasping and desperate it must have seemed.

And now this—

I would have to speak to Mr. Darcy and return his gifts.

This had gone too far now.

"Lizzy, are you quite all right?" Kitty asked. "Is it not what you wished for?"

"I— It is," I said as I pulled the paper away from the parasol to examine it more carefully.

It was a delicate trifle, with pink satin ribbons and a fringe of intricate lace at the bottom. It was not a parasol for walking in the rain, but a parasol for walking through a London park... or for flirting with gentlemen.

"It is lovely," I added as I handed it to Kitty.

Lydia ran her fingers over the silk ribbons. "But you do not even like pink, Lizzy. Does Mr. Drummond not know that? Will you send it back?"

"No, I will not send it back," I sighed.

"Then will you let me borrow it?" she asked. "I should very much like to walk through town with it. Mr. Denny will compliment me for certain—"

"He compliments you anyway," Kitty muttered. "If you do not want it, Lizzy, may I have it? As a wedding present?"

It was difficult to deny my sisters anything, especially now. But I had to return it to Mr. Darcy.

"I shall make a decision later," I said. "Go and show it to Mama. She will be very pleased to see that Mr. Drummond has sent me a proper gift."

Lydia pulled the parasol from Kitty's hands and raced down the corridor toward the parlor. With an indignant cry, Kitty followed her at a similar speed and I pressed my cold palms against my cheeks and took a deep breath.

I could not bear this any longer.

We all, even Jane, expected that Mr. Bingley would propose

any day, but it seemed most likely that he would make use of Lady Lucas' upcoming dinner party to do so.

He had already come to visit Papa on three occasions, and each time he had departed with a smile upon his face. My mother's attempts to force my father into revealing the topic of their discussions was, as usual, in vain, and the house was in no small amount of uproar over it.

Though, to be fair, it was a quiet sort of uproar.

Kitty's own wedding was fast approaching, and my mother's attentions were drawn in far too many directions for her to focus upon one thing.

My mother's exclamations from the parlor solidified my decision. I would have to confront Mr. Darcy and tell him that it was time to abandon the ruse.

This had gone on for far too long already.

I had prepared a letter from Mr. Drummond that would end our engagement. It was secreted inside my writing desk and hidden under my bed. When the time was right, I would reveal it and all of the lies and deception would be over.

But I had to speak to Mr. Darcy... sooner than later.

∾

The opportunity I had been hoping for did not occur until the day before Lady Lucas' dinner party, and I was convinced that everything would go awry.

Jane was, once again, invited to Netherfield Park, but this time, instead of going directly to the parlor, she walked the gardens with Mr. Bingley. Caroline and Louisa complained bitterly about the chill in the air, but I found it invigorating and welcomed the change of pace.

Mr. Darcy had been cajoled into joining us, and I found the opportunity to walk close enough to him so that we might speak without being overheard. I did not wish for Caroline to become suspicious, so I would have to speak quickly.

"You have gone too far, Mr. Darcy," I said.

"Too far? How so?"

"The gifts," I said.

"Was there something wrong with them? Did you not like the book? I had it sent from Pemberley— Bryon is one of my particular favorites. That work is of singular value in his catalog... I expect great things from him in the near future. That is, if he can avoid personal destruction—"

It was far too tempting to continue the conversation, and the revelation that he enjoyed Byron's work struck me in an odd way but I tried to shake it off.

"I— It is not that."

"Then what is it?"

"They are too much," I managed. "The parasol—"

"My sister, Georgiana, picked it out," he said. "Is it not to your liking?"

"It is... It is beautiful," I said. "But it is... it is entirely improper—"

"Is your Fiancé not to send you gifts?"

"He does not exist," I hissed. "So, no, he should not be sending me gifts!"

The gentleman's chuckle sent a shiver down my spine. "I see. And what shall I do, instead?"

"Does Mr. Bingley plan on making an offer of marriage to Jane?"

He seemed taken aback by my question. "He does."

My heart pounded in my chest as I looked at him, but his expression was unreadable, and his dark eyes met mine without hesitation. "He has told you?"

"He has."

"Then there is nothing more that you need do," I said. "As soon as their engagement is confirmed and announced, then I shall receive a letter from Mr. Drummond breaking off our arrangement."

"And what reason will you give? I daresay there will be many who will be dumbfounded that such a perfect match should end so suddenly."

"Perfect match," I muttered. "Indeed, the only perfect man for me is one that I have conjured from my own imagination. I should not be surprised by that."

We walked in silence for a few moments and I smiled as Jane leaned her head against Mr. Bingley's shoulder.

"Mr. Drummond will, regretfully, end our engagement as he plans to stay permanently on the continent. Traveling frequently with no house or estate to settle at for any length of time. It would be a life that would not be suitable for a wife. Or a family."

"I see."

He shook his head, and I was struck by the disappointment in his expression, but he said nothing.

"Do you think the reasoning is unsound?"

"No, indeed," he said. "What young lady in search of a happy marriage would wish for such a thing."

"I shall return the book and the parasol as soon as I am able," I said.

"You shall not. They were gifts. I hope that you will keep them and appreciate them in the spirit that they were given."

I swallowed hard and tried to push away the strange feeling in my chest that had sprung up at his words.

The spirit in which they were given.

"Then I suppose we shall have to end our association," I said finally. "I will have no further need to continue this falsehood. But you must promise me that you will say nothing— To anyone."

"If you think it prudent."

I straightened my shoulders and wondered why I felt strangely at his agreement. "I do."

"Then your secret will be safe with me," he said.

"Charles, I am freezing," Caroline complained. "Must we walk in these gardens forever? I demand that we go back to the house at once!"

Mr. Darcy nodded as I lengthened my stride to catch up with the others. I was distracted by the good-natured argument that took place between Caroline and her brother which finally ended in an agreement that we would all return to the house.

When I turned to look back at Mr. Darcy, I found that he was no longer walking with us. He had disappeared into the gardens, or perhaps he had gone to the stables instead. Whatever the reason for his departure might have been, I wondered if I had been the cause of it.

Surely, he would be happy to be rid of my tiresome requests and the fiction that I had brought him into...

At the same time, he had not requested the return of any of his gifts and I wondered at the regret and disappointment that I had seen in his eyes.

But he had confirmed that Mr. Bingley intended to make an offer of marriage. Jane would say yes, of course, and all of my problems would be solved in a heartbeat.

Eleven

Lucas Lodge was an old estate—one that had been gifted to Sir William and his family when he had acquired his new title. As grand as this change in situation had been for the Lucas family, the acquisition of Lucas Lodge had come with its own set of challenges. Challenges that Lady Lucas spent a great deal of time lamenting to anyone who might be willing to listen. And even those who were not.

The house itself was massive, and in serious need of repair. The furnishings were outdated and dark, and there were several rooms that were unable to be used because of leaks or holes in the plaster.

When Charlotte had shown me the house I had been astounded by the dilapidated condition of the property and its sad state of disrepair.

I could not imagine the cost of keeping such a place in good order, let alone to make the necessary repairs. Which was the cause of much of Lady Lucas' moaning and complaints.

But such things would not stop Lady Lucas from inviting anyone of consequence to a dinner party. The house had a large ballroom which had been repaired well enough to justify a celebration.

Lady Lucas never shied away from decoration, and as a result, the ballroom was filled with overstuffed furniture, card tables, and masses of silk and velvet draperies covered the outdated wallpaper and shabby window sills.

"One would think that they would be more concerned with the upkeep of their estate," my mother muttered as we entered the ballroom.

"I am sure that they have their hands full," I said. "Maria has just been presented and I am certain that Lady Lucas will wish for a prudent match—"

"Indeed," my mother huffed. "A wealthy match, to be sure. Not every mother can be as fortunate as myself. Three girls engaged, and I feel certain that Lydia will not be far behind!"

She sighed happily and I did not feel the need to remind her that Jane's engagement had not yet been announced. If an offer had been made, Jane had been tight-lipped about it, but there was, indeed, something different about her. She smiled more often, and there was a pink flush to her cheeks whenever Mr. Bingley's name was mentioned.

I was overjoyed for my sister, but I would say nothing until the engagement was official.

As for Lydia, my silly younger sister could not decide on any one gentleman, so it was impossible to say whether or not she would ever secure an engagement—or if she would ever be happy with just *one* admirer.

Musicians had been set up in one corner and I rolled my eyes to see that Lydia was already pestering them to play songs that she liked and could dance to. After supper, there would be dancing until very late, but Lydia never wanted to wait for anything.

Caroline Bingley and Louisa Hurst were already in attendance, and Mr. Bingley had already found Jane. They spoke together near the great fireplace, and my heart swelled to see the sweet smile upon my sister's beautiful face as she looked at him.

But Mr. Darcy—

Had he not come? The disappointment I felt was far too keen. I was worried that he had taken my request to end our association far too literally. Was he now avoiding me?

"Miss Bennet—"

I turned in surprise to see the gentleman standing just behind me.

"Oh! Mr. Darcy—"

"Did you not expect to see me here?"

"I confess I was not certain that you would attend. I thought that you disliked such events—"

"Mr. Darcy does, indeed, abhor all social gatherings."

Caroline Bingley's smooth voice and catlike smile chilled me as she approached.

"Caroline," I said. "It is wonderful that you are here. Lady Lucas will be thrilled—"

"I am certain she will be," Caroline said in a bored tone. "I must admit that I am quite surprised that Mr. Darcy was so eager to attend this gathering tonight. More often than not he must be cajoled and begged to drag himself to such things. In London he often wishes to do nothing but sit in the drawing room and read. He is very tiresome."

"Indeed," I murmured. I had half-expected to learn that the gentleman was fond of the club and card tables, but Caroline had ruined that image of him very quickly.

"It is no crime to prefer my own company and the words of the great authors of the world," Mr. Darcy said. "Though you do delight in chiding me for it."

"No respectable gentleman should shun social gatherings," Caroline said with a sharp smile. "But this brings me to another topic—about another gentleman."

The chill returned with alarming speed as Caroline turned her pale eyes to me.

"Oh?"

"Mr. Felix Drummond. Your fiancé."

I took a nervous sip of my punch. "What about him?"

"His office in London was on South Street, was it not?"

I nodded. "Indeed that is what he told me."

"Well, I have written to a friend in London, merely to mention that happy news that one of my dear friends was newly engaged to a lawyer who held offices on South Street, and she was very surprised to hear it. Can you guess why?"

"I— No, indeed, I cannot."

"Well, Miss Eliza, it is because there are no lawyers with offices on South Street."

I did not know what to say and I took another sip of punch. It was heavily mixed and the taste of the rum was strong on my tongue.

"What is your point, Caroline?"

Mr. Darcy's tone surprised me, and I glanced at him, wondering what he might say. He had promised—

"My point, Mr. Darcy, is that Mr. Drummond has lied to you, Eliza. Does that not bother you?"

"I—"

"Or, what is a much more troublesome outcome, is that Mr. Drummond does not exist at all. I have tried, in vain I might add, to write to Mr. Drummond's partners in London, but he does not seem to have any, and no one has heard of him..." Caroline paused to determine if her words had had any effect on me, and I bit down hard on my cheek to keep from saying anything I would regret.

Although, I would be lying if I did not admit to myself that I regretted so much already...

"Well?"

Caroline looked at me expectantly, and I wished that I could run from the room and return to Longbourn to await my eventual ruin as she told the entirety of the guests about my falsehoods.

"Caroline, you are quite correct," Mr. Darcy said.

Caroline's eyes widened. "I beg your pardon—"

"No—" I whispered, but Mr. Darcy raised his voice and continued to speak. Heads turned and I felt my cheeks grow hot.

"It was a cunning deception," he said. "Elizabeth Bennet conspired to fabricate an engagement—"

This was it. I was ruined. We were, all of us, ruined.

"What are you saying?" Caroline exclaimed.

"It was false," Mr. Darcy said. "A false engagement. Mr. Drummond does not exist."

"Lizzy!" My mother's voice echoed in the ballroom as she stormed toward us. "You cannot be— Is this true?"

"I am afraid so," Mr. Darcy continued.

"What is the meaning of this?" my mother cried. "Lizzy— You will tell me at once! Mr. Drummond sent you letters, and gifts!"

"They were all a falsehood," Mr. Darcy answered for me again. "The letters. The gifts. They were all from me..."

There was a collective gasp from the people who surrounded us, but none of them looked as shocked as Caroline Bingley.

"It cannot be—"

"But, indeed, it is," he replied. "Miss Bennet and I conspired together to keep this charade."

"But to what end," my mother demanded. Her voice was dangerously loud, and I knew that it would not be long before she burst into hysterical tears.

"To disguise the truth of our own engagement," Mr. Darcy said. He reached out and took hold of my hand. "I could not allow it to overshadow Mr. Bingley's courtship of Jane Bennet, and so we agreed to keep our meeting, and our love a secret until Charles and Jane could announce their own happy news."

I almost dropped my glass of punch as the gentleman's fingers closed over mine.

"I—"

Mr. Darcy looked at his friend. "Is this not true, Charles?"

"It is, indeed," Mr. Bingley cried. He pulled my sister toward the crowd that had gathered. "But there is no need to keep your secret any longer. Jane has agreed to be my wife, and I am the happiest man in all of England."

Applause broke out in the ballroom and my mother let out a shriek of happiness that echoed above the applause.

I watched in silence as Mr. Bingley led Jane onto the dance floor.

I ought to be happy. I ought to be happy. I should have been the happiest of all, but all I could think of was the way the gentleman had stood before me and the way his hand had closed over mine—

Caroline Bingley's cold glare burned into my back, but I could not look at her, and I would not allow myself to care what her opinions might be.

"Lizzy— we will speak about this," my mother said as she rushed toward my father. My father's smile warmed me just a little as he raised his glass of wine toward us, but I could not shake off my utter surprise.

Caroline Bingley was obviously just as stunned, and I could not mistake the choked noises she made as Mr. Darcy pulled me across the room.

"I must speak with you," I blurted out as I tried to pull my hand from his grasp. But he held my fingers tightly.

We escaped the room, pausing only to accept the well-wishes of the guests who had overheard what he had said.

In the corridor, I wrenched my hand out of his grip.

"What is the meaning of this?" I blurted out.

Mr. Darcy's smile made my heart lurch in my chest.

"Whatever do you mean?"

"I mean, what are you doing?"

He reached for my hands, but I took a step back.

"You have ruined me," I said.

He shook his head. "I have not. Listen to me."

"I cannot—"

"You must hear me," he said. "I love you—"

"I cannot believe you would do this," I muttered as I backed away, but he reached out and grabbed my hands.

And then it finally registered. He had said— But how—

"I do not believe it," I choked out.

"How can you not? I have read all of your letters—the letters that you said yourself have been made up from your own imagining of the gentleman who would be your perfect match."

"I do not understand—"

"I felt that in reading those letters that you had seen into my very heart," he said. "Everything you described, it was my own life laid out on the page. Some of the details were, of course, incorrect, but I felt as though you knew who I was... without even meeting me."

"I—"

"I was intrigued," he said. "You were so unlike the ladies I had known before. They had been lovely, and proper, but they had no fire in them. No imagination. But you... I could hardly think of anything else. How alike we were... As such, I agreed to assist you with your plans."

"I do not understand—"

I took a deep breath and looked into his eyes. There was a gleam of hope in their dark depths that I could not ignore, but I could hardly allow myself to believe that he would ever care for me.

"At first I found myself jealous of a gentleman who did not exist, but then, as I read the letters, I realized just how deeply you yearned for someone different. Someone like me."

I did not know what to say, but I knew that my mother would demand an explanation.

"Is this a ruse as well?" I asked. "Is this engagement nothing more than words to distract from the lies I have told? The lies that I have made my sister, my father, and you tell over these past months?"

"It is not a falsehood," he said softly.

I could not look at him.

I turned away and looked down the corridor, desperate for an escape. My mind whirled with confused questions, and the possibility that he was, indeed, correct. I had been searching for something—and I had found it, quite by accident.

I expected him to grab me and force me to turn to him. I expected him to reach for me and pull me into his arms. I expected him to hold me and kiss me... but instead, he stepped back.

"Elizabeth— I hope that you will find it in your heart to realize that I am right. You know that we belong together."

"And what if you are mistaken?"

He smiled. "I know that I am not."

I gnawed on my lip and clasped my hands at my waist, unsure of what to do with them or how to stand. "And what would you have of me," I demanded.

"Before this night is over, I must have your answer."

"My answer?"

"Yes," Mr. Darcy said. He reached out and touched my cheek and I did not flinch away. "I would ask you to be my wife. I have already spoken to your father, but he warned me that his permission meant nothing if you refused my offer..."

Of course my father would avoid the responsibility of this moment. He had always said that he would trust my judgment when it came to my choice of a husband. He had never disappointed me.

"Did he?"

Mr. Darcy nodded. "Indeed, he made it very clear that his opinion on the matter was meaningless."

"Hmm."

"You do not have to answer just—"

"I will," I said.

His dark eyes widened. "You... you will?"

I smiled at him then and stepped closer. "I will be your wife."

His hand was warm in mine, and he held it gently as he moved closer.

"You did not have to help me," I said. "But you did— Jane has everything she has ever wanted. I did not believe that the gentleman I had always dreamed of existed... but here you are."

"Elizabeth, I—"

But I did not wish to hear him speak any more. I tilted my chin up, hoping to encourage him. Thankfully, he realized what was required and he smiled as he bent his head to kiss me.

The very deepest love did not have to begin perfectly.

In fact, it was in the moment that I had given up in the search for it that it had found me... Perhaps that was the perfection of it.

THE END